Publishers Note

This is a work of fiction. Names, places, characters, and incidents are the product of the author's imagination or are used fictitiously, and any resemblance to actual persons, living or dead, business establishments, groups, events, or locales is entirely coincidental. Library of Congress Cataloging-in-Publication Data-Conover, Anne Veronica Hierholzer

BOOK NAME: ESCAPE to FLAMINGO

(2019) ISBN 9781793924995

January 18, 2021, ISBN: 978-1-7357631-2-5

Update June 5, 2025

ESCAPE
to
FLAMINGO

AUTHOR

Anne Veronica Hierholzer
CONOVER

For
Gary Bartholomew, whose stories of his
youth gave inspiration to key aspects of this
story.

TABLE OF CONTENTS

ESCAPE
TO
FLAMINGO

CHAPTER 1

"Florida Dog Days," Dannie Hurricane Dove Macon, better known as HD, whispered to himself. The high school senior sat in the back of the bus and endured the hot, humid summer air and bus fumes that blew into his reddish tan face.

He daydreamed of being accepted into Graham-Rutherford University in Daytona Beach, Florida and was anxious to hear back from them. He imagined the look on his mother's face after she read his acceptance letter, complete with a scholarship award in aeronautic engineering. He was almost certain of the scholarship. Then, he would move away from this place and, perhaps, his parents and little sister would come with him to Daytona too. He wanted them to get out of Florida City and—the violence.

HD reeled at the memory and flashbacks of a shooting at school that killed some of his classmates. He desperately wanted out of the school before it happened again, which was all too possible. HD was in class when the shooting started. Within moments, the shooter was at his

2

classroom door and a spray of bullets zinged overhead. Terrified, everybody hit the floor and hid under their desks. One seat away, a fellow classmate lay dead. HD reacted quickly. He grabbed his cellphone from atop his desk and amid the shots, he dialed 911.

Five high school seniors died that day. Distraught over the horrendous attack on the kids and especially his son, HD's father spent a week in ICU from a near fatal heart attack. "Bad times," HD said and counted the days to graduation as the bus sped down Tamiami Trail.

The distraction of the scrubby edge of the glades, palmettos, palms and underbrush that teemed with unseen snakes, reptiles, and other wildlife, proved to be a bit of a reprieve from the school shooting. HD recalled the Burmese python that he and his cousins caught last winter, whoa! What an exciting day—and they got paid for killing it too! The Everglades once belonged to his ancestors and still do as far as HD was concerned. In his heart the Glades will always be his people's land.

HD turned away from the window and looked toward the two other kids whose bus stops were coming up. They too rode quietly and endured the heat as he did. HD was the first student to board the bus in the morning and the last to get off at the end of the day.

CHAPTER 2

Jack Weller, a seventh grader, sat in the middle of the bus and threaded nylon fishing line through the eye of a fishhook. The fishhook was one of three for which he traded his three Iron Man comic books.

"I love to fish," Jack said to himself. He imagined his boat on the river, and his next catch. Fishing was always in the forefront of his thoughts. While there was no dislike for school, his current fishing trip daydream came to a screeching halt. "Jack," his teacher called out in a loud voice tone, "copy down the final exam assignments I've written on the blackboard!" Jack mumbled a quiet complaint to himself as he reluctantly got back to work.

However, while riding the bus home, his mind roamed freely. He carried on imaginary conversations with his dad. "School will be out soon and then watch out fish! I gotta get home and take the boat out on the river, ain't that right, Dad? Imagine discovering a new fishing hole deep in one of the tributaries that flow to Florida Bay. I can just see us casting out a fishing line—and within seconds, I snag a huge toad fish, and there you are Dad, right beside me, pulling in a big bluegill. Oh, yea man. Oh yea, now that's some action," Jack exclaimed as he glorified fishing with his dad, "Yep, that's right, we spend the day fishing then sell our catch of the day to the locals. We save the fish money for a vacation. Oh yea, you betcha'! Then—Florida Keys here we come! I can see it now Dad, out there on one of those charter fishin' boats pullin' in the big ones!" The gangly seventh grader's thoughts filled him with joy.

Jack's bus stop was the second to the last. Even though the heat was oppressive, on this leg of the route all was quiet on the bus. The rowdies, all the loud talkers and bullies had been dropped off and now it's a quiet ride home and Jack was lost in his euphoric fishing thoughts.

He resented the teacher's interruption of his daydream today because his imaginings kept him from spiraling into a hole of sadness and loneliness that bespoke the reality of his life. He could barely get past the truth of it, but he knew with the promotion to the next grade and then high school he'd be old enough to be on his own and that gave Jack hope. He smiled as he successfully threaded and knotted one of the hooks. He had a little more time to daydream before he got off the bus. Jack put his fishing hooks and spool of nylon fishing line away and prepared himself for the walk home from the bus stop.

He'd walk the half mile down a sandy dirt road to his house, which was located behind the tropical scrub of Homestead's southernmost neighborhood. Routinely, he kicked an empty whiskey bottle down the road, or some other discarded bottle or can. There was always something that littered the side of road.

Yesterday was trash day and as usual all the garbage was put out along the curb and often overflowed into the road. However, the trash men never picked up anything thrown beyond the garbage cans. Jack recalled how the sheriff deputy cars were parked a few houses up from his home. Blue and white lights flashed back and forth on the hood of their vehicles. Jack wondered what was going on over there.

A yellow tape had been stretched around an area in the road where several deputies stood. Another deputy was bent over with a plastic sheet, that covered something that lay in the road. A tiny hand peeked out from under the sheet. At first Jack thought it was a doll that the police were looking at, but as he got closer, he got a glimpse of a little hand palm up on the asphalt, it could only be a baby. "Damn," Jack thought, "who would throw away a baby?!"

Neighbors were nowhere to be seen; in fact, it was unusually quiet as Jack walked past the yellow crime scene tape where the tiny baby lay dead in the filthy street. Again, Jack exclaimed, "Damn, who would throw away a baby?!"

It was too much for Jack to contemplate or comprehend that a baby lay dead in the street. He blocked it out of his mind with thoughts of an imaginary fishing trip, he and his pretend dad would take in August.

CHAPTER 3

Eight-year-old Billy Culpepper sat in the seat
behind the bus driver. He played with a brand-
new red yo-yo that he'd won in the second-
grade spelling bee. "Won't momma be proud of
me," Billy thought to himself. He continued
with the yo-yo until the bus ride lulled him to
sleep, which occurred just about the same time
every day. Even today with his new yo-yo to
distract him he became drowsy and dozed off
just as he pocketed the yo-yo. As always, he
would awaken to the sound of the bus driver's
voice, "Billy, time to go."

His mother always waited for the bus at the
intersection of Tamiami Trail and the road to
their subdivision. She always had the car
running with the AC cranked up to full blast
against the heat of the day. Today, the sleeping
second grader had been dreaming of diving into
the clear blue water of their swimming pool
when the bus driver called his name. She looked
back at her small passenger through the rearview mirror and envied the mother of the
adorable child.

****

9

CHAPTER 4

Here I am, Sarah Miller, a retired U.S. Army Sergeant. I have recently returned home from two tours in Afghanistan. I was stationed at the Nangarhar Province, Jalalabad. I drove supply trucks, mail trucks and a variety of military vehicles that included Mine-Resistant Ambush-Protected (MRAP) gun trucks. The supply and mail trucks always brought news from home and lifted the moral of soldiers.

I drove thousands of miles across the barren lands of Afghanistan, proud to be part of the bigger picture, part of the solution towards peace. Some trips required days of preparation and were dangerous. I often repeated a phrase, *"stay alert, stay alive,"* a command that I learned from my superior officer.

I was a good driver and a crack gunner too. My years in the Army taught me that I could sleep any place and I learned to fall asleep at the drop of a hat. I had hoped for a career in the military. I look back and marvel at the courage and bravery I had back then, especially when my convoy got ambushed. One never expected to be in an ambush or get shot even though we're trained for it. A bad hit was something I didn't think about until I was in the thick of it. I took a tough hit to my leg, an injury that put me out of the military.

I limped away from the army with an honorable discharge and into the loving arms of my husband, a military officer, with six months left of his deployment abroad. We planned a bright future and made wonderful plans. We were only married a year when he took a street bomb to his face in Jalalabad. Now, I am a widow, grateful to be employed—as a school bus driver. It's not exactly what I had in mind when I left the Army, but I enjoy it.

I carry a concealed weapon. Of course, had I asked my employer permission, they would have said no and, it probably would have shed suspicion over my stability as a bus driver even though I am the furthest thing from crazy.

Driving a school bus is easy. I drive precious cargo back and forth from school, instead of being on the constant lookout for snipers, or ambushes. Even still, I holster a weapon on the job. Maybe I'm a bit over the edge. I must confess, I'm a PTSD wounded warrior widow.

I try not to think about *that* when I'm driving the bus. Sometimes, out of nowhere, my eyes well up with tears. That's no good since I've got to see where I'm going. On other occasions, I catch myself driving the bus down Tamiami Trail a bit over the speed limit. I don't need speeding tickets, I need this job, so I reserve my mourning for the evenings when I can drown my sorrows in a bottle of chardonnay. I looked back at Billy one more time and smiled and wished he was my little boy.

CHAPTER 5

Twelve months earlier, Kyle Moleto, Eddie Ringold and Ben Sykes graduated from North Florida University. Today, Kyle leaned against his car, arms crossed, impatient and annoyed. His buddies were late for the trip home. Just as he was about to call Ben, he showed up.

Together, they waited another ten minutes before Eddie arrived. When Eddie did show up, he was breathless because he had run across campus to meet his friends, "Sorry I'm late, had to return my apartment keys to the landlord and tie up a few loose ends before he'd give me back my deposit."

"Let's go," Kyle ordered as he got into the driver's seat. Without another word, Eddie and Ben threw their bags in the back of the jeep. Within minutes, Kyle was on I-95 heading south to Florida City. "I'm gonna miss this town," Kyle said. The college grads laughed knowingly. "Who's to say we can't continue our thrills when we get back home? I mean Eddie and me gotta have a little action or we'll die of boredom in Miami, right Eddie?" Eddie said nothing. "You know, Ben you're right, as far as

13

I'm concerned," Kyle said, "crime not only pays, but it is also the thrill of the century and better than sex, drugs and booze all together."

Kyle and Ben laughed but Eddie just stared out the jeep window. Eddie pretended to be preoccupied with the scenic views of miles and miles of Florida pine trees along the interstate highway.

"The last two college semesters were amazing," Ben said, "why me and Eddie stole and sold and stole some more throughout the last nine months of our senior year. I think that makes us smokin' smart and between the three of us, we managed to cash in over fifty grand and that was just *petty* theft." Kyle looked out the rearview mirror at Ben, "Well, then let me lay out my most recent plan for the three of us. You know Ben, with your mechanical expertise, Eddie's construction know how, and my smarts, I am convinced we can knock over a bank and I just happen to have quite a plan."

Kyle presented his ideas to his buddies and by the time they arrived at Ben's place, sixteen hours later, they had a plan. As far as Kyle was concerned it was perfect. Two weeks after graduation and after all the family welcome home dinners and congratulatory graduation parties were over, the three college grads planned their first major bank heist.

"Okay guys," Kyle said, "we start by casing the banks in the area, beginning with our hometown, Florida City. Next, we head to Homestead, and finally, while a bit over the edge for first time bank robbers, we case a few banks in Miami that I think will be easy pickings."

Eddie was hesitant to move forward with the idea of a bank heist, "Look Kyle, there are cameras everywhere and armed security guards which makes bank robbery a bit more difficult than petty burglaries and small-time thefts."

"All the banks are free standing buildings," Ben said, "except one, an older bank in Florida City that joins side to side to another building. The other side of the bank is a vacant lot, construction wise, the Florida City bank in my opinion, Kyle, is the best target."

"I hoped to do a bank in a better area," Kyle said, "but I'm not going to argue with the facts so—yea, I'm in. Now, first I need to get a closer look at how things get done inside the bank. I am going to apply for a job as a bank clerk, then I'll study the layout and day-to-day routines. I also plan to work my way into the vault, where the customer safe deposit drawers are kept. It'll take some time, maybe a couple months, but patience will win out I am sure of it."

"So, Ben said, "that means Eddie and I have to get a job while you are casing the bank, right?"

"Yea, Ben, I guess so, I mean we want to do this right don't we? Look at me Ben, I mean I'm handsome, charming and confident. I can gain my boss's trust."

As planned, Kyle got hired at the Florida City Bank. Each day he compiled a list of bank details. Several months later, he shared his findings with Ben and Eddie over dinner, "I know where the bank's cash is stored, where important bank officials work, where the cameras are located, who the armed guards are, their shifts, and the area where bank officers assist the safety deposit customers. We're getting close."

Kyle patiently bided his time at the bank. Twelve months into his employment, he was granted special clearance to assist customers, "Guys I have access to certain areas of the vault's blind camera free areas. It is a happy day guys, a happy day!"

"Does that mean you can see the cash?" Ben asked.

"No, not yet, my every move is securely monitored on the security cameras where the large bags of cash are stashed. Getting past the cash room cameras is a problem. I think now is the time for you and Eddie to help figure out how to shut the cameras down."

"Kyle, I know you pride yourself on patient planning and so far, it's paid off, but Eddie and I, on the other hand, we are not so patient. I am not living with rich parents like you are right now. My upstanding well- respected long-time residence of good ole' Florida City parents, are dead and have been since I was a boy. I gotta do better than my older sister, Peggy Sue, who gets a pittance for what she does for a living, you know? She's always telling me the same story about her profession every time I see her, overseeing the county school systems computer programs and equipment that monitors and records activity on school buses. She loves her work! Takes pride in heading up the program and the safe environment that the surveillance cameras assure drivers and children and, blah, blah, blah. A good family reputation is just not enough for me Kyle. I want what we had at college, a steady life of interesting heists. I have an insatiable appetite for this business. We had quite a thing going besides our studies, right Eddie?"

"Yea, Ben we had quite a thing going. But for me, this is it, when this bank heist is done, I'm leaving town. I got no one; no sister, no rich parents, no one in the world. In my opinion, meaning no disrespect to you guys, I must move on and, like I said, this is the last job."

Secretly, Eddie knew how stupid it was to continue hanging out with Ben and Kyle, but he couldn't resist the thrill of stealing stuff and all that cash—he kept telling himself that this will be the last job, and then he'll disappear, never to see Ben and Kyle again. Hopefully, separation from Ben and Kyle will assuage his burden of guilt.

Eddie had not quite gotten over his father's death. Captain Edward Ringold died while Eddie was in college. He was a good man, a war veteran, a man of honorable character and the only good influence in Eddie's life. When Eddie thought of his father, he was ashamed of himself for what he had become and all the petty crimes he'd committed. Now, he agreed to do a bank heist with Ben and Kyle. "No more after this, Kyle," Eddie said, "I made a promise to my dad."

"Well, I'm anxious to get on with it," Ben said, "however, my patience is wearing thin. Me and Eddie have spent this year working in retail warehouses supplementing our meager pay with stealing from the stores and anyplace else that's an easy mark. Luckily, we have not been caught, not yet anyway. However, the owners did become aware of recent thefts and beefed-up security, even in the employee rest rooms. This made stealing stuff almost impossible so, yea Kyle, I am getting a little impatient here."

Weeks later, Kyle contacted Ben and Eddie, "It'll be a clean, smooth operation. Here's the plan; there is no alley between the bank and the building next to it. Therefore, we can access the bank through the vacant building's basement wall that joins the bank's basement, then locate the vault's safe deposit area where there are no cameras. We break through the basement ceiling. Once in, Ben, disconnect the security cameras in the rest of the vault, I'm confident you can do that, right?"

"Yep," Ben nodded

"Meanwhile," Kyle continued, "I'll ask for extra desk work such that I can stay late and surreptitiously observe who might be working late hours. I've already observed that several loan officers have after hours appointments with some customers. Sometimes they stay until eight o'clock in the evening. While the bank is not officially open to the public after five o'clock, it is open to some bank executives and exclusive customers. The night guards come on duty around nine o'clock. So, I figure, we should break into the bank after midnight or so. Meanwhile, Ben, you and Eddie start work on the wall that the bank shares with the adjoining building. Once you guys are through the basement wall, we cover it up. It's a great plan and I don't know about you two but, I am anxious to get started."

CHAPTER 6

One oppressively hot day in June the bank air conditioning system broke down, and all the employees were sent home until the repairs were completed. Kyle was ecstatic, "I can't believe my luck! The din of noise of the ongoing bank repairs will cover Ben and Eddie breaking-in through the adjoining basement wall and then through the vault floor—today we rob the bank!"

With a pickaxe and sledgehammer Ben and Eddie broke through the circa 1868 old-style vault floor. For some reason, the current standards and designs required by the Treasury Department were never implemented or perhaps overlooked at the Florida City Bank.

"Take as much as you can carry, maybe five or six large canvas bags of cash and slip out through the vault floor," Kyle ordered, "then through the hole of the basement wall, into the vacant buildings' basement and into my jeep."

All this they did in broad daylight under the cover of the noise and distraction of the bank repairs. After they loaded up the jeep the three thieves drove away without incident.

When Kyle arrived at work the next day the bank was crawling with the police. The bank manager appeared to be in a conference with several businessmen that Kyle didn't recognize. He and all the other employees were shepherded to a large conference room on the second floor where they were individually called and questioned by the police.

Kyle appeared calm and sincere during the interview as he expressed his concern for the bank and its depositors, "Like I said, officer, I didn't notice anything unusual when I left the bank the day before the bank closed for repairs. I went home, like everybody else."

The police accepted Kyle's statement even though he had no alibi, as his parents were out of town. Exhilarated, Kyle laughed and chuckled all the way home. A myriad of thoughts raced through his head as to what he was going to do with his share of the money. Conversing with himself, Kyle said, "What a rush! It just doesn't get any better than this. Of course, I will have to remain at the bank until everything settles down and then I will resign my position at the bank but, for now I must concern myself with getting my share of the money to a good hiding place. There's that place my folks vacationed when I was a kid. A camp and fishing place. It's vacant and deserted now. Nothing much left of it except a run-down Marina. Shouldn't be a problem though."

Kyle recalled when the National Everglades Park officially declared the town of Flamingo, located at the southernmost tip of Route 6336, a ghost town. He was just a kid when the rest of Flamingo's campgrounds had been beaten to smithereens during several consecutive hurricane seasons. So much so that the National Everglades Park (NEP) decided it wasn't worth rebuilding. Kyle was suddenly beside himself, "I think I might have a terrific hiding place for my share of the money—only forty miles from home. Life just keeps getting better and better," he mused.

The bank closed for three days. During that time, the three thieves implement the next phase of their plans. "I say let's take the money to your apartment in Miami, Ben. There we can count it out and split it three ways."

"How are we going to get it there?" Eddie asked.

"Well, I can remove my spare tire and we can pack the six bags in the spare tire space of my jeep and together we all drive down to Ben's place, what do say Eddie?

"Fair enough, then you, me, and Kyle, come back home together, right?"

"Yep."

Kyle removed the spare and set it against the wall of his garage which at the time seemed like a good idea. However, while on their way to Miami the left front tire blew out a short distance from Flamingo Road. Kyle slowed the jeep and pulled over to the side of the road. The blistering heat and hot, humid westerly winds greet the three men as they got out of the jeep.

Cars zoomed by and blew dust and wind in their face. "What a stinking mess this is turning out to be," Eddie complained, knowing full well that the spare tire leaned against the wall of Kyle's garage. "Kyle, there's no way we can make it without another tire. One of us will have to catch a ride into town and get a new one.

Can't call a tow truck because we can't risk the money being discovered," Ben exclaimed.

"Keep your shirt on!" Kyle hollered back.

"Okay then you two go and I'll stay here," Kyle said angrily. Ben and Eddie looked at each other, a sudden feeling of distrust came over them.

"Why don't we all just stay here, wave a car down, knock the guy out and take one of the tires," Ben blurted out sarcastically, "we could steal his spare!" Wouldn't that be more like the college grads that we are?"

"Calm down Ben, you sound like a maniac," Eddie said, "look, we be polite, not draw attention to ourselves, we're intelligent guys, come on now, we've come this far, what say we flag down the next car and offer to buy their spare tire," Eddie said, trying to be the diplomat, "what's the matter with you guys, nobody steals someone's spare tire!"

"So," Kyle said, "we all stay here, because we don't trust each other enough for one of us to hitch hike into town, buy a tire, take a cab back and then put the new tire on. Am I right?"

"Yep," Ben said as he glared at Kyle.

"Well, we better try to flag a car down and offer to buy their spare tire, which I think is stupid!"

No one stopped for them even though the hood was up, "What if the police drive by or what if a well-meaning driver calls the police and reports a car on the side of the road," Eddie said.

As Kyle, Ben and Eddie debated over the chance of that happening, a school bus stopped at the stop light, at the intersection of Flamingo Road and Route 41, a short distance from the jeep and across the street from the Tamiami Gas and Shop.

CHAPTER 7

When I pulled up to the traffic light, I noticed three young men in a heated conversation and a jeep that appeared to have a flat tire.

"From the way these guys are fussing, I bet they don't have a spare, " I say to myself, "I'm not at liberty to give the boys a hand, not while driving the school bus, besides they're old enough to take care of themselves. Hmmm, my military training to "give aide" is tugging at me. Anyway, I'm sure they know that picking up anyone except the school children is against the rules." Considering I was stopped at the traffic light I couldn't help but glance over at the men and the disabled green jeep. The last thing I expected was for the men to look back at me and when one of the men approached the bus, I hoped the light would change, but it is one of those three-minute red lights with a turn light before my lane got the green again.

I pretended not see one of the young men walk up to the bus doors. When he tapped on the doors I turned and shook my head no.

"Sorry I can't open the doors," I said in an officious manner. I made a point to avert my eyes and not look at the man at the doors. I turned towards the traffic light. The man tapped on the doors again. I turned back at the man, "I said I can't"—the barrel of a handgun was pressed against the double glass doors and pointed at me.

"Open up," he said. I shook my head no, the young man cocked the gun and pointed it at me again, "I said, open up," the guy's deadly glare was fixed on me. I looked up at the large mirror in the center of the bus window and glanced back at the three boys. HD was looking straight ahead, watching me and I know he heard me talking to someone outside the bus. I turned my head away from the man with the gun and said loud enough for the kids to hear but not so loud that I could be heard outside the bus,

"BOYS! GET DOWN AND HIDE." I reached back and felt my handgun strapped against my rib cage. Slowly I opened the doors and put my hands up. I glare at the man with the gun and said nothing.

"Ma'am seems we have a flat tire here, and we don't have the spare," the man said as he waved his gun and motioned for me to move, "get up and go sit right over there, where I can see you." I moved across the aisle opposite the driver's seat and sat down. The two other men boarded the bus, and when the light changed the driver with the gun put the bus in gear, drove through the intersection and turned right onto State Road 9336, Flamingo Road.

The hijacker drove about a quarter of a mile then pulled over to the side of the road, turned the bus off and opened the bus doors.

"Get out," the driver said to me, again as he waved his gun. He turned around to see if there are any kids on the bus. Fortunately, the boys must have hidden, as the bus appeared to be empty. I backed away from the bus as far as I could without being swallowed up by a thick tangle of thick palmetto scrub along the side of the road. The three men followed me out of the bus.

"Look I have a cell phone let me call a tow truck for you," I offered.

"She says she has a cell phone and will call a tow truck for us," one of the men replied sarcastically. "You idiot, what are we supposed to do with the bags of money if a tow truck takes the jeep to the repair shop?" The driver hissed back at the other man.

"Then we can call my sister Peggy Sue, she'll keep her mouth shut, if she knows what's good for her. I'm not happy with you waving a gun around Kyle," the man said. The man with the gun called Kyle walked over to me, a big smile on his face, a third man followed behind.

"Hey Ma'am, uh let us make the call I'll give the phone right back to you," Kyle said in a charming voice.

"That won't be necessary, I can dial it right here for you," I said as I reached into my jeans pocket and pulled out my cell phone.

"I believe I just asked, if I can make a simple call on your cell phone, I promise I'll hand it right back to you," Kyle insisted, a grim look on his face. He pointed his handgun at me again. The third man backed away from Kyle and said, "Whoa Kyle!"

I took advantage of the other guy distracting Kyle and made a run for the bus, but he was too fast for me. He grabbed me by my hair, dragged me off the bus steps and threw me to the ground. I landed face down, sand clung to my face and mouth. Suddenly, I'm back in Afghanistan, I rolled several times away from the men. Within seconds I'm back on my feet, pulled out my handgun and held it with both hands, took deadly aim at my assailant, my arms outstretched in front of me.

"Whoa, whoa!" said Kyle "I'm sorry I'm sorry, just got a little carried away, we just want to make a call on the cell phone, is that too much to ask?"

"Let's put the guns away, I understand that you have kids to take home, right?" Kyle said.

I catch myself before I blurt out that there are three kids in the bus, "The bus is empty, asshole."

"Well, that's even better," Kyle said.

I should have shot the jerk when I had the chance the authorities would have said it was self- defense, but no, I relaxed my hold on the gun and for a split second I thought the guy named Kyle with the gun could be rational. What a mistake that was, in a flash he raised his gun and shot me. I staggered back, the wind knocked out of me, a searing pain shot through my chest, and I fell to the ground and dropped my handgun.

"Look what you made me do? We don't want any trouble here, we're not bad people," Kyle said a smirk spread across his face.

I pressed my hand over the wound, a red stain bloomed on my chest, my hands came away bloody. I raised up and feebly reached for my gun.

"Don't even think about it," Kyle growled as he kicked me hard in the head several times before everything went dark.

**

"Damn that felt good," Kyle said as he looked down at the unconscious woman. Blood dribbling from her mouth. He picked up her gun and threw it into the tangle of scrub palmettos along the side of the road.

"You idiot!" shouted Eddie, "What are you thinking? This is not what we're about, since when do we shoot people?" Without missing a beat Kyle announced, "We must get rid of her. Quick, help me get her in the bus before anyone sees us." Without another word the three men picked Sarah up, carried her into the bus and dump her on the center aisle as though her body was nothing more than a sack of potatoes.

"If she wakes up, which I don't think will happen anytime soon, I'll have to kill her," Kyle threatened, "now we go back to the jeep, put the bags in the bus and we drive to my hide out." Ben and Eddie looked at one another, "Your hideout?" Ben said sarcastically.

"We'll talk on the way," Kyle said, "now let's get outta here."

All Eddie could think about was how this was not supposed to happen, "I want out," Eddie said under his breath, "Kyle's bad news and there's just too many surprises. It's bad enough to contend with his smart-ass rich kid attitude, now this. I'm not going down for murder for anybody."
Oblivious to his buddy's reactions, Kyle said, "After we get the money to the hide-out, we'll dump the bus in a lake, then walk back to the road and hitch a ride home." Kyle drove the bus back onto Tamiami Trail, made a U-turn at the traffic light and pulled up behind the jeep.

The three hijackers transferred the money bags from the jeep to the bus and tossed them down the aisle not far from where Sarah lay unconscious.

Then, Kyle drove the bus onto the highway and turned right, onto State Road 9336.

"Where are we headed?" Ben asked.

"I told you, to the hide-out, not far from here." Kyle growled. Eddie sat quiet for a few moments, then said, "Hurricane Alley."

"What?" Ben asked.

"Hurricane Alley," Eddie repeated, "this road leads to an old Marina, a ghost town and a torn up deserted campground. A slew of hurricanes ripped through it some years ago. Florida State Parks won't restore it because of the catastrophic storm damage. They're afraid the place might get hit again. It seems to be a magnet for hurricanes."

"Yep, that's right," Kyle said, "and that's why it's considered an official ghost town."

"They have a Marina," Eddie said, "I hear the place is still operational part of the year, did you check and see if it's open, Kyle?"

"The Marina's not open, not in the summer, Eddie," Kyle said, an edge to his voice. Ben sat a few seats behind Kyle, a scowl on his face, visibly unhappy about the latest developments; they just hijacked a school bus, Kyle shot the bus driver and intends to murder her. Now he just found out that Kyle has a hideout. Ben looked over at Eddie, "Did Kyle say anything about a hideout to you?" Eddie shook his head no.

"I thought we were going to split the money three ways at my place and be on our way," Ben whispered, "the hideout is certainly not part of the original plan. I wonder why Kyle didn't tell us about the hideout until now." Eddie leaned over and whispered back to Ben,

"Shooting a bus driver and kicking her in the head is certainly not part of the plan either."

Thirty-five minutes later, Kyle pulled up to the deserted Flamingo Visitor Center, across from the Marina. Vines crawled up the sides of the building and mildew blackened the faded pink stucco walls.

"Wait here," Kyle said, "let me check out that upper room. I'm quite sure this place is abandoned."

Kyle got out of the bus and climbed a set of stairs attached to the outside wall of the Visitor Center that led to a crusty, rust eaten, and weathered metal door. Kyle pulled out a skeleton key and jiggled it in the lock until the door screeched open. The room was dank, dark, and empty. He leaned out the door and shouted down to Eddie and Ben, "We'll put the bags in here."

They gathered the bank bags and stored them in the vacant room. "This is all we had to do," Kyle said, "but no, that woman pulled a gun on us, it's all her fault. Now listen up, dead or alive we've got to dump her body and the bus in a lake just a few miles from here."

"Not to change the subject, but when were you going to tell us about the hiding place, Kyle?" Ben asked. The two men glared at each other a second too long, then Kyle blinked and said, "I didn't have a chance to tell you guys about this, everything happened so fast. Besides this is where I planned to take my share of the money in the first place."

"Why don't I believe you?" Eddie said, a growing suspicion in his voice tone, "I have *plans* man—plans that include splitting the money at Ben's place, and then we all go our separate ways."

"Let's get going," Kyle ignored Eddie's complaint, "we don't need to be out here in the dark, this area has some real big, nasty bugs and critters that come out at night."

The three college educated thugs got back on the bus and headed back the way they came. Kyle drove ten miles then turned left onto Bear Lake Road. "This'll take us to a lake where we can dump the bus. No one will ever find it, we'll just drive into the lake, with the body in it. The End." Kyle said, as though he was talking about launching a canoe.

There was no lake at the end of the paved road. Instead they were at a turn that led to an overgrown trail marked by a sign that read, *Bear Lake 2 miles*. Underneath was another sign that that read, *No Motor Vehicles Allowed*. The trail to the lake was nearly invisible; tropical foliage grew over crushed limestone and shells which obscured the trail. Large thick roots bulged out of the path like the knees of a giant whose body was buried beneath the trail. "Okay, let's go, might have to take it a little slow to the lake," Kyle said as he turned the bus onto the trail.

The bus screeched against a tangle of branches and heavy brush. Vines tangled around the bus wheels and were sheered out by the roots. Every now and then the bus jolted up and down over the thick heavy protruding roots in the path.

When they got to the brackish lake, Kyle put the bus in neutral. Eddie and Ben jumped out, and just before Kyle jumped out, he looked back at Sarah just in case she had become conscious, but she was gone. He jumped off the bus as it rolled quietly into the lake.

The men watched as the bus slowly descended into the deep brackish waters of Bear Lake. "She won't get far, not with a gunshot wound and bleeding out, she won't last the night," Kyle said to himself. He decided to keep Sarah's disappearance a secret from Ben and Eddie. They were suspicious of him enough already. "Let's get outta here," Kyle said as he walked ahead of the other two men. "Ms. Bus Driver's survival is slim to none and that is okay with me," Kyle mumbled to his ruthless self, "everyone knows the stories about being lost in the glades—no one survives. If the crocs, alligators, or bobcats don't get her, the boa constrictors, pythons or anacondas will, or other ground critters. Then of course, everyone knows the stories of the "Unseen." The old timers' stories of American Indians who live hidden away in the glades. If they find you, lady, you'll never get out alive. No, she's not going to survive."

"Okay, listen up guys," Kyle announced, "it's a good fifteen miles back to the main highway. We can mosey along but I'm jogging my way out of here before the sun sets. The sooner we get out of here, the better. The money's in a safe place and we all know where it is. So, let's get back to the car and get it in the shop."

The men jogged down Bear Lake Trail towards the paved road. Kyle was delighted with himself. A delicious sense of power pumped through his body as he recalled how clever he was in the bank robbery. "The way I see it, despite the minor shoot out with Ms. Bus Driver, we were able to hide six canvas bags of money in a perfect hiding place. We'll all get back to civilization before dark." Kyle boasted, "yes! It's turning out to be a successful day after all."

As the hijackers jogged up the trail, Kyle looked passed the thick tangle of trees and foliage. "An impressive hiding place," Kyle thought to himself as he peered into the glades, "that woman is nowhere to be found and that's good. The deeper she goes into the glades the worse it will be for her."

CHAPTER 8

HD looked up when Sarah said to hide. He
quickly scanned the bus and saw that the two
other kids had not responded. He hunched over
and quickly ran up the aisle out of sight of the
bus's double glass doors. A chill ran up his
spine when he saw some guy pressing the barrel
of a gun against the bus doors. It was aimed at
the bus driver. HD grabbed Billy, who was
asleep then ran halfway down the aisle and
tagged Jack Weller to follow him. Hunched over
they ran to the back of the bus.

HD arranged the boys in a hiding position
near the exit doors, behind the last passenger
seat on the left-hand side of the bus. Startled
awake with all the moving around Billy's eyes
widened with fear. HD put his hand over Billy's
mouth, set a finger to his own lips, looked over
at Jack and to them both he whispered, "Stay as
still as possible, don't make a sound."

HD listened carefully to a man who was
shouting at the bus driver. He overheard him
give orders to Sarah to get out of the driver's
seat and sit somewhere else. HD then heard two
additional male voices after they boarded the

bus. HD peeked up and saw a man with a gun take over the driver's seat. He drove the bus a short distance passed the traffic light and turned onto another road. HD was familiar with the next road up from the light and was relieved that the bus was going away from Miami.

The strange men argued and within minutes the bus slowed and pulled over to the side of the road. The driver ordered the bus driver to get out of the bus. At this point HD could only hear muffled voices. Then, a gun went off. The high school senior overheard the men shouting at each other. One of the men was named Kyle, another Ben and the third man was called Eddie. The three men were angry, and shouted at each other, but HD could not make out what they are saying. Minutes later they boarded the bus still shouting and angry. Then, HD heard a loud thud, something had been thrown down the aisle of the bus. One of the men shouted orders about going back to the jeep and picking up bags of money.

Lying flat on the floor, Jack could see the men's shoes as they walked up and down the aisle. He also could see the bus driver lying on the floor about fifteen feet from where he and the other two boys were hiding. He turned and whispered to HD, "I think they hurt Ms. Miller! She's lying in the aisle! She has blood on her clothes and face."

As the bus jolted forward and pulled out onto the highway, the three terrified boys lay still as death. HD thought frantically of ways to get out of the bus. Jack wanted to scoot forward to see what was happening.

"Don't do that," HD said, "they might see you in the rearview mirror. Then we're all dead."

HD knew the area well. His family had a long history in Florida City that went back a couple hundred years. He also knew that the bus turned onto Flamingo Road, just past the traffic light, then shortly after the turn onto Flamingo Road the bus slowed then turned 180 degrees and pulled over to the side of the road again.

The men argued with each other as they went back and forth from the jeep to the bus. They threw canvas bags down the aisle near where Sarah lay in a crumpled heap. Once the bags were loaded, they got back on the bus and drove onto Flamingo Road. This time they didn't stop and pull over to the side of the road, this time they kept going.

HD knew that located at the southernmost tip of the park was Flamingo, the only town on this road. It was what the man meant when he said Hurricane Alley. Anyone raised in the area knew about the ghost town called Flamingo and that it was devastated by recurrent hurricanes and subsequently closed by the Everglades National Park.

HD's heart raced. He recalled the shoot-out at the school, and now this. The hijacking of the bus terrified him. The kids were crunched up behind a seat hopefully hidden from the armed robbers. He reached for his cell phone which was usually in his back pocket. Today however, he'd put it in his backpack and the backpack was several seats up from his hiding place.

HD felt a sense of dread come over him and he feared for his life and the lives of the other two boys. He wondered if the bus driver was dead. "What's your name?" HD whispered to the seventh grader.

"Jack Weller, what's yours?"

"Dannie Macon, but you can call me HD, everyone else does."

The bus engine made enough noise that HD could no longer hear the men talking and figured the bus noises would muffle his voice too. "Look Jack," HD said in a low voice, "I want you to scoot under the seats until you can see Ms. Miller's face. See if she's conscious, call to her in a whisper."

Without a word Jack slowly crawled under the bus seats to where he could see the bus driver's face, luckily her face was turned in his direction. The front of her shirt was blood stained. Her eyes were nearly swollen shut. Blood trickled from her mouth, her face and neck were bruised and swollen. "Ms. Miller," Jack whispered against the rumbling of the buses' engine. He called out to her a couple more times, and just before he decided she might be dead she opened her eyes and looked at him. Jack motioned shh with his finger to his lips. Sarah Miller looked at him for another few seconds and slowly closed her eyes. Jack whispered, "Don't move." He then crawled back to HD, "she's alive."

"Okay, we sit tight until the bus stops again. I think they're heading for Flamingo," HD whispered. He checked out the bus exit door. It opened with a single latch and when it opened, it swung wide and outward. HD wondered what kind of noise the door would make and whether they could get out without being seen.

The ride continued without incident for another forty-five minutes. Finally, the bus slowed and turned off the asphalt highway onto an off- road sandy place and came to a stop. The double glass doors swished open, and the men got off the bus. Their voices faded in the distance. HD carefully looked up from where he was hiding and watched the men disappear behind the side of a faded pink and white stucco building. They'd arrived at the old Flamingo Visitor Center, now abandoned since the last hurricane. HD knew that another six miles south of the Center were the abandoned Flamingo campgrounds. "Let's get out of here," Jack pleaded.

"Not yet, it's all open spaces, they'll see us in a second," HD warned, "we wouldn't get a hundred yards, and they have a gun. Besides, we can't leave the bus driver." While the men were busy casing the abandoned Visitor Center, HD crept up the aisle passed the bus driver to where the canvas bags were stashed. One of the bags lay partially opened. Hundred-dollar bills bound in tape were visible. HD pushed the bags closer to the front and away from the bus driver. He then quickly checked how she was doing, but before he could say anything to her, he heard the men's voices in the distance and hurried back to his hiding place with Jack and Billy. The men boarded the bus and each grab two bags of money, one of the men shouted orders.

"When they all leave with the money that's our chance to get her back here," HD whispered, "it's the only chance we have to save her life."

"What if they notice her body's missing?" Jack asked.

"I doubt it, they're pretty occupied with the money." HD said hopefully.

"We should drive the bus back to Tamiami Trail and call the sheriff," Jack insisted.

Meanwhile, the men were on their way to the Visitor Center to stash the bags of cash. While the men were gone Jack crawled up the aisle and checked the bus console for keys, but the keys were not in the ignition. "I think when the time's right we might be able to escape through the exit door without them seeing us." HD said. Then, he and Jack gently carried their wounded bus driver to the back of the bus and carefully maneuvered her such that they could ease her out of the back-exit door.

HD was sure that the men planned to ditch the bus with the bus driver in it whether she was dead or alive. He also assumed they thought that she was the only one on the bus. Yes, they'd probably pick a place to dump the bus, but where? Or maybe they planned to torch it, but that would leave a mess and bring the park rangers. No, they're going to hide it somewhere in the glades, probably in one of the brackish lakes. HD knew of several places close to the Wilderness Waterway off the main road, further in the glades.

When Kyle, Eddie and Ben returned HD overheard where the driver wanted to dump the bus and HD's hunch proved correct, Bear Lake which was at the end of Bear Lake Trail. HD knew then that was where they would try to make their escape. Kyle drove back down Flamingo Road and onto a side road. HD was certain the bus was on Bear Lake Road.

At that point the back of the bus became increasingly hot, and the air was stifling. The boys were drenched in sweat and nauseous from the smell of fumes. Despite the miserable ride, the bus driver remained unconscious, her face swollen, her blouse a bloody mess. HD worried that no matter how careful they were, she might cry out or moan anytime and alert the men. Billy held her hand and waited for HD to tell him what to do. HD refused to abandon their bus driver, the idea of leaving her behind was not an option. He must try and save her too.

When the bus turned left again, HD knew they were on Bear Lake Trail. The wildlife, Semaphore Cactus and tiny Thrinax Palms had overgrown the unused footpath. The roots of the Gumbo Limbo and Cardinal Pine trees protruded from the limestone path like large and jagged fingers. Decayed broken trees, whose split trunks and roots ripped from the ground by successive hurricanes lined the trail, leaving long expanses of the path unshaded.

Kyle slowed the bus so he could better maneuver through the rugged foot path that had never been a road for motor vehicles, let alone a large school bus. As the back of the bus consistently rose and fell with a bang, HD knew *now* was the time to jump. He slowly opened the exit door and held onto the door latch, to prevent it from swinging wide and bang against the back of the bus.

Jack jumped out first then wrapped his arms around the bus driver as HD lowered her onto the footpath. Next, Billy jumped out and HD followed close behind. He ran to keep up with the bus long enough to secure the door with a gentle push. Billy scrambled to the edge of the path and into the brush. HD and Jack gently pulled the bus driver into the brush too. Together the three kids dragged the woman as far from the footpath as they could to assure safe coverage from the men. God forbid they discovered she was missing and then come looking for her. With their bodies pressed hard into the soft damp ground the bus driver and the three school children lay still and quiet.

Meanwhile, the three men sunk the bus in the lake at the end of the path. The engine died as it sunk into the brackish lake. HD and the others heard the hijacker's voices coming towards them as they walked back towards Bear Lake Road. Their voices grew louder as they passed by where the kids were hidden. No one dared move until the three would be killers' voices faded in the distance.

HD wondered if the men noticed that the bus driver's body was gone. When HD no longer heard the men's voice's he decided to move everyone deeper into the glades. Just to be safe. At the right time, HD planned to double back to Bear Lake Trail and get as close to the lake as they could. HD was sure that the men would not return. The glades were not the best place to be in the dark and they seemed to be all about the money.

HD came across an opening in a small grove of Gumbo-Limbo trees. Beyond the opening was a large mound of discarded shells that according to HD's grandfather were used as tools. Some of the shell mounds in the glades dated back thousands of years. HD's familiarity with the shell mound, was because the trail runners of his community considered it a hunter's landmark and that was why HD knew they're not far from the lake.

The bus driver and kids rested in the cool shade of the trees until HD was sure the kidnappers were gone. Then it would be safe to double back to Bear Lake Trail. Slowly, HD carried the wounded woman through the tangle of tropical plants and trees. Her arms hung limp around his neck, and he stopped often to rest. Hard as it was, HD was determined to make it to the lake. He blotted out any fears of who or what they might encounter along the way. Billy trailed behind holding tight to Jack's belt loop.

CHAPTER 9

HD had a lot of things to consider, to survive the night. It would be pitch black in about five hours. He scanned the humid, thick tangle of trees, vines, and woody shrubs as they trudged back to Bear Lake. HD was confident the authorities were out looking for the missing bus. His father was probably sitting on the front porch wondering where he was. Billy Culpepper's mom always waited for him at the edge of the road. No one was ever at the bus stop for Jack, but surely his folks would be concerned too.

"Okay, let's take a break," HD said. He and Jack slowly lowered Sarah down on the ground against a huge Gumbo-Limbo tree as easily as they could. She was conscious now but too woozy to talk and whimpered in pain.

"I'm gonna look around and see if I can figure out where we are," HD said and disappeared into the thick foliage. Meanwhile, Billy sat down and rested his head on his knees. The bus driver looked over at him and motioned for him to come sit by her. She held out her hand which he eagerly accepted, sat beside her and leaned against her good side, the side without a gunshot wound.

"I'm afraid and I want to go home," Billy whispered. Too weak to speak the bus driver nodded sympathetically. "I hope he comes back," Billy whimpered in his little boy voice, "I've never been in a place like this, I think we're lost."

"We're not lost, you'll see," Jack whispered as he stood up.

He scanned the glades for the three men. Jack was just too skittish and afraid to sit back down. He was certain that they were being hunted. How could the hijackers have not seen that the bus driver was no longer in the aisle? He was convinced somebody noticed.

HD appeared out of the thick tangle of glades; his bare chest glistened with sweat. He'd removed his shirt and tied the sleeves together to carry thin branches of green fern, purple beauty berries and needle leaves full of white blooms along the stems.

Twisted dangly strands of roots poked out of the top of his shirt. He knelt on the cool sandy earth, opened the shirt and sorted through the weeds and berries.

"We can't get to where the bus is dumped because the mangroves are too thick through here," HD said as he continued sorting the array of medicinal herbs and flowers, "so we should go back around the lake to the trail which is about a ten-minute walk. I was able to see the westerly sun through a clearing near the Wilderness Waterway. We need to go east. Once we get back on the trail, we can make a fire. We'll have dryer open ground on the trail than we have here. We need the dry ground to get a fire going before dark."

"How're we gonna make a fire?" Jack asked, "I don't have anything except a spool of nylon string and a couple of fishhooks."

"We don't have any camping gear, either. All's I got is my yo-yo," Billy said as he opened his hand, to reveal a red yo-yo set in his palm.

HD remained silent, as he stripped leaves from the stems of a beggar tick plant, sifted through the small mound of leaves, and discarded bugs and other debris before he crushed them into a lump of mashed greens.

"Ma'am, this will help with the pain, it should be applied around the bullet wound," HD said gently.

"Why would I trust this high school senior?" The woman thought to herself, and barely paused before she said, "Do it, I'll take whatever you've got and call me Sarah." HD sat next to Sarah and slowly peeled away the sticky, blood drenched shirt far enough from her wound to smear the green mash around the bullet hole. Sarah lay back and closed her eyes. HD then turned to the stash of stems, flowers, and leaves and held out a handful to Billy and Jack.

"Here, these are edible, it's not much but it'll get us through the night." HD gathered the rest of the weeds, and greenery and bundled them back into his shirt.

"Ms. Sarah, we should be going now." HD said, then he and Billy carefully helped her to her feet. As they trudged east towards Bear Lake Trail, HD reached into his pocket and held the tribal flint arrowhead his father gave him and that his grandfather had given to his father. Some might say the arrowhead was a good luck charm, but it reminded him of his identity. He knew how to survive in times like these, in the everglades, in the heat of the summer. The flint arrowhead in his pocket will spark a fire tonight, a campfire and deterrent from the night predators.

"I can do a lot with my knife," he told himself, as he anticipated a night in the glades. Weapons were not allowed at school and HD knew that. But he rationalized his knife strapped to his leg as his defense against the kids who come to school and flash their own weapons at each other.

HD never showed his knife to anyone or flashed it around school and would never brandish it unless his life was threatened. The memory of the school shooting was still very fresh in his mind and with the level of violence now prevalent in the schools, he was ready for dangerous bullies, he would not be a victim. Like his forefathers, he'd take a stand and win.

HD led the way to Bear Lake Trail. Together with Jack they staggered through the formidable roots in the trail and dragged Sarah between them, Billy tagged along, his fingers tightly gripped on Jack's belt. Finally, they reached the lake and the trail dead ended. This was where the bus was abandoned and, where tire tracks ended at the edge of the lake. HD set Sarah down about fifty feet from the water's edge. The hot gritty limestone/shell trail scraped Sarah's hand as she tried to sit up.

"You alright Ms. Sarah?" Jack asked as he and HD set her down on the trail.

****

I grunted a response in a faraway voice. I was consumed with pain. My face throbbed, I could hardly see anything, my ears rang, and a dull constant pain owned my head. I took short shallow breaths. I knew I had been shot and the pain pierced me. I don't know how many times I blacked out and I have no idea what is happening. "That man, Kyle," I moaned, "if I get out of this alive—I just might sleep forever—just like in the war—only I didn't sleep forever, did I? Stay alert, stay alive." I said to myself...

Sarah keeled over. "I think she blacked out again HD, what should we do?"

"Just let her be for now, Jack. She needs to rest I'm sure she's in a lot of pain."

Within an hour of their arrival on the trail, the sun set behind the trees and cooled the limestone trail. HD could do no more for Sarah and felt helpless. He feared for her life.

"Getting hijacked is a pretty crazy way to get to know each other." Jack and Billy nodded in agreement. "Until the authorities find us, we must figure a way to survive the night. Jack, did you say you have some fishhooks?" HD asked.

Jack reached into his pocket and pulled out a small clear plastic box with the two fishhooks and a little spool of nylon fishing line. "Traded my favorite comic books for these hooks."

HD pulled his pants leg above his knee and unstrapped his hunting knife. He then strode several yards into the trees, cut two long branches off a young Gumbo-Limbo tree that grew next to its' gigantic parent. Its massive roots grew under and over the trail. HD made a small gash at the end of each of the limbs and tied a piece of Jack's nylon fishing line to the tip of the branch.

"Here's one fishing pole. Jack, see if you can get the string and hook on the other, then, check out the lake and see if you and Billy can catch a fish or two. Be careful, keep a look out for gators and snakes."

While Sarah lay slumped over on the now shaded trail, HD walked around the edge of the trail; pulled up the roots of dog fennel and collected dry limbs and bark that had fallen under the giant Gumbo Limbo tree. He gathered as many dead tree limbs that he could hold; dry dead limbs, dry dead roots of dog fennel and the red tree bark were sure to burn. HD gathered enough limbs and bark to keep several fires going all night.

Meanwhile, Billy and Jack took their handmade fishing poles to the lakes edge and baited their hooks with worms they dug out of the thin strip of shoreline. HD looked over at them and hoped they'd catch a fish or two. Even if they don't at least the two boys were distracted from the terror of the day. HD made a small mound with the dry woody kindling and set about striking a spark with his knife against his flint arrowhead. Five strikes into the effort a spark caught and lit the brittle kindling. He then delicately fed the tiny flame until it burned steady on one of the larger limbs.

The evening was heralded with the endless, frenetic cricket chirps that competed with croaking frogs and the loud, buzzing, clicking sounds of the Anhinga night callers. These noises were just the beginning of the nocturnal sounds of the everglades. At least with the fire going they won't be huddled together in the pitch black as the sounds of the glades were formidable. With the firelight they'd be able to see the flying night critters coming at them or the creepers before they crawled down their pants or into their shirts.

Still, HD had work to do. He made sure he had enough purple beauty berry leaves left that he had gathered earlier still balled up in his shirt. He hoped to have enough to crush and smear on everyone's arm, legs, neck, and face before dark. He crushed the leaves until his hands stained green. "Hey look what we caught," shouted Jack, "last thing in the world I ever thought I'd be doin' today is catchin' me a fish!" Billy and Jack held up their lines, each boy had hooked a peacock bass that squirmed frantically against Jack's fishhooks embedded in their mouths.

"At first I thought it was some monster fish, and it scared me, but Jack says it's just a ole' peacock fish," Billy exclaimed.

"Yea, I recognize them from pictures I saw in a fishing magazine." Jack said excitedly.

"I never heard a' such a thing as a peacock fish," Billy laughed.

HD skinned and gutted the fish then skewered them through with a stick. "Now, you hold it over the fire 'till it's done," HD instructed, "you can tell it's done when the meat flakes away from the stick."

"Save a piece for Ms. Sarah," Jack said, as he noticed that she had come around again. Billy approached Sarah with a piece of cooked fish, "Here you go, Ms. Sarah, its fish me and Jack caught and its good!" Sarah took the piece of fish from Billy and winced as she tried to nibble on it. "We need to get ready for the mosquitoes," HD said as he smeared the sticky, mashed leaves of the purple beauty berries over the exposed skin of his body and face. Jack and Billy followed suit and HD smeared the make-shift repellant on Sarah as well, "This stuff will help keep the bugs away."

Before the evening light faded to a pitch black and while they all sat around the fire, the mosquitoes came out in full force. "Jack, I need you to help me set two more additional campfires, we have a center campfire which is ours for the night. The second fire is over there about twenty feet in front of us, and another about twenty feet behind us, all in the center of the trail."

Jack and HD built woody mounds and with a burning branch from the center campfire they lit two additional fires. "It's gonna be a long night," HD said to no one.

The thought of the glades catching fire crossed his mind, a spark from the campfires could land in the thick glades. It was critical to their survival to have the other two fires because they would keep bold night predators at bay. That way HD knew he would have a fighting chance to defend against whatever might step into the light. The fires were critical in the pitch black of night, in a place like the glades, in the heat of the summer.

HD planned to stay awake all night and hold vigil against the night stalkers. He'd tend the fires the way his dad had done when he was a young boy. HD recalled the family camping trips. Camping trips that were never during the heat of the summer. The importance of why his father stayed awake all night on their camping trips hit home this night. If his father could do it, so can he.

CHAPTER 10

After Kyle fitted his jeep with a new tire, he drove home to his parent's house. After graduation he balked at his parent's insistence to live at home until he settled into his profession. His parents were surprised and disappointed that he settled for a job as a bank loan officer at the lower income end of Monroe County. They wasted no time telling him that their brilliant college grad son could do so much better.

The *che che che* sound of the lawn sprinklers greeted him as he made his way to the front door. His parents had driven down to Key Largo with some friends for the week. The long walk from Bear Lake Trail to his jeep parked near Tamiami Trail left Kyle exhausted. His face, arms, and neck sported a tender red sunburn, hot to the touch. He showered and changed his clothes, then padded out to the kitchen in his bare feet and set the AC to 69 degrees, turned on the ceiling fans and poured himself a hefty glass of bourbon.

Kyle sat down at a table that faced floor to ceiling glass doors that opened to a spacious brick patio, complete with a built-in grill and a twenty-five-meter swimming pool. A good size pool for a private residential home. It was too hot for Kyle to sit outside even though there was an evening breeze. So, he sipped his bourbon and stared out at the glassy clear pool where the reflection of the setting sun lent tiny sparkles of light that danced on the water.

Kyle was beat and too tired to think, other than to say, "Tomorrow will be a better day." Instead of the smooth burn of the bourbon and the view of the tranquil pool washing away the edgy and restlessness of the day, Kyle obsessed even more over the bus driver's missing body. He kept telling himself that the glade's creatures would get her before morning and make short work of her body. It never dawned on him that she just might survive, not until now.

"Besides," Kyle repeated to himself, "everyone knows the stories. Of course, some people think urban legends are nonsense. But people have been known to disappear in the glades. No one gets out of the glades and it's not just the glades and gators or big cats, it's those people that live in the glades the '*unseen.*' Everyone in Monroe County knows the stories but some people think it's all folklore. Well, I believe the urban legends. That woman will not be alive in the morning, nope, she is dead meat, and I will not think on this anymore."

Kyle dismissed any more thoughts of the bus driver, whom he mercilessly and repeatedly kicked in the head and then shot. He decided he'd think about tomorrow, "I'll report to work tomorrow, as usual, draw no attention to my wonderful self, and just be cool."

When Kyle arrived at the bank the next morning several of his fellow employees were gathered around the front of the bank. On the glass doors a sign was posted:

The bank is closed to the public. All employees must report for an important meeting at 8:30am today.

"Okay," Kyle says to himself, "I'm here, now what?" After all the employees were gathered in front of the bank, one of the senior officers unlocked the doors and let everyone enter the bank lobby where metal chairs had been set out in neat rows. The employees were asked to take a seat. Once everyone arrived and was seated, the bank President took his place at a podium set up in front of the employees.

*****

"Good morning, everyone. I'm Mark Corman the Bank President." Corman appeared calm, friendly and was dressed in a fine business suit. However, he was far from calm. He feared he would lose his composure and become hysterical. Indeed, the Bank President was having a difficult time controlling a creepy kind of hysteria that was bubbling up inside him. His head had a way of trembling when he was upset. His mind was awash with ugly thoughts, "An employee sitting in front of me, someone looking back at me, robbed my bank and if I had a gun, I would shoot them all dead, because someone among them thinks they are going to get away with it and everyone else hopes they do—no, no I can't think like that I have to remain calm," he chided himself.

He took a deep breath to control the urge to vomit all over the podium before he introduced FBI Agent George Russell.

The agent showed up yesterday and told Corman, "The FBI will take it from here, Mr. Corman, there is no question in my mind that the robbery was an INSIDE JOB; and everyone is suspect, even though the initial interrogations have proved otherwise."

Russell announced to the seated bank employees, "Yesterday, 1.2 million dollars were stolen from the bank vault."

Kyle stopped listening to Agent Russell after he announced how much he, Ben and Eddie, took away in the six canvas bags. Kyle nearly fell out of his chair. "This is awesome! Wait 'till I tell Ben and Eddie," Kyle said to himself. "What a haul, this is huge!"

His heart pounded in his chest. He breathed deeply and slowly to keep from appearing overly excited. However, the joy of it all slowly dissipated by the time Agent Russell had finished talking.

Now, Kyle Moleto thought how stupid they were for robbing the bank. The only thing he and his buddies could do with the bank money was hide it or bury it indefinitely. Agent Russell folded his arms across his chest and stood with his legs splayed out like a soldier at ease and said, "Every merchant in the nation knows that large conspicuous purchases with large amounts of cash are called into the police. The merchants will make the sale alright, then they turn right around and call it in. The same applies to a bank teller who gets a cash deposit over ten thousand dollars. That money is automatically reported to the US Treasury Department. Less than ten thousand is considered suspicious and goes on a suspicious activity report better known in the bank world as SAR."

In closing, Agent Russell announced in a mildly threatening voice tone, "The robbery is being looked at from every angle, but we believe that this is an inside job, and all employees are suspect. No one can leave town until further notice."

On that sour note, the employees were excused for the day and told to report to work tomorrow, business as usual. Kyle broke out in a sweat. Never in his life had he been unsure of himself or had ever exhibited lack of control until today.

As he drove home, his clammy hands slipped around the steering wheel. He pulled over twice to vomit on the side of the road and by the time he pulled into the driveway, his voice was hoarse from screaming at himself all the way home. He hurried into the house, ran to his room, fell on his bed and commenced to scream some more into his bed pillow. By the time Kyle pulled himself together, the sun had long set.

"I got this, I got this," he repeated over and over. He had several ideas, and he talked them out loud to himself, "The first thing I do is dress in black, wear gloves and a mask, yea, then I go to the Flamingo Visitor Center pick up the money take it back to the bank and dump all the bags at the front door. I know if I can pull it off, there's a chance I won't get caught."

Kyle had accepted this failure; it was difficult because he's the heist boss and he should've known about the FBI, and that they would be the lead agency involved in a bank robbery. "This is all my stupid, stupid fault, but I am going to fix it. If Ben and Eddie get in the way well—I'll just kill them."

CHAPTER 11

Meanwhile, Ben and Eddie were at the Tropical Canteen in Coral Gables having drinks. The sound of kettle drums pulsed through the bar. People on the dance floor bobbed up and down to the rhythmic beat of reggae music. It was a happy place, and Ben and Eddie enjoyed the ambience, the music and dancing people.

Ben looked over at Eddie and asked, "Have you heard from Kyle today?" Eddie shook his head no and said, "Word is, the FBI is investigating the bank robbery. The news reported that they considered the bank robbery to be an inside job." Eddie and Ben look at each other then they burst out laughing. "Well, Eddie, that gets us off the hook!"

"Unless they finger Kyle and he turns states witness and reports us as accomplices Ben, then it's not so funny."

Their smiles faded away and their laughter turned into grim silence. "Kyle didn't tell us about the hideout."

"No, he didn't, and I'm sick of waiting, I made plans, Ben."

"Look," Ben pleaded, "I think we should go get our money, we split it three ways and just get out of here."

"How do we split it; there's six bags?"

"We each take two bags and leave two for Kyle, believe me, Eddie, Kyle knows how many bags we hid."

"We'd have to weigh the bags, you know, in our hands, make sure they all weigh about the same, best we can do." Eddie said, trying to put a fair edge to splitting the money bags three ways. Ben rolled his eyes, "Fine, we'll weigh the bags."

"I say we go out there tonight, Ben, if we wait any longer the cops will be swarming everywhere, it's all over the news now."

"Okay Eddie, I tell you what, we meet at the Flamingo Visitor Center, tonight at 3am, whaddya say?" Ben and Eddie shook hands, gulped down the rest of their drinks and left the Tropical Canteen. Ben dropped Eddie off at his apartment on his way home.

With stolen money from previous heists Eddie had stashed away, he was able to pay in advance for a short-term apartment lease.

Except for a box of clothes, a large canvas duffel bag and his mattress, the apartment was empty. The rest of his things were stored in a locked storage unit a couple blocks from his apartment. "Keep it simple," his father used to say.

Eddie tried not to think of his dad. He had been a good man, a decorated war hero. "Oh Dad, maybe if you were still alive, I wouldn't be tangled up with the likes of Mr. Know-It-All Kyle," Eddie complained to no one. He felt ashamed and bad about himself. He knew his father would not have approved of his friends and bank activities. He also knew better than to blame his father's death for his life as a thief. Death is what it is, taking the good with the bad.

If it hadn't been for his war hero dad, Eddie's college education would have never happened. His father made sure there was plenty of money set aside for Eddie's college education. Eddie tried not to think about his dad—he promised himself he'd start over, and, with the heist money, he'd do good things.

Eddie stuffed all his clothes and anything else that would fit into his duffle bag. It was midnight now, and from his place it was a two-hour drive to the Flamingo Visitor Center. He had time to gas up his white, late model Silverado truck, get to the ATM machine, empty his account, and grab some provisions at the all-night grocery store. As he drove to the Visitor Center he again thought of his father, "Yea Dad, I'll do good things with the money, and no more heists, that's a promise."

***

Ben, on the other hand, was in a mood, and as he drove back to the Visitor Center, he talked aloud to himself, "It was supposed to be a smooth heist. I'm not happy with Kyle and KYLE'S way of doing things," Ben said sarcastically, "I have had enough of his arrogance. I could kick myself for getting involved with him in the first place, geez what was I thinking—all that wealth he has, who wouldn't be drawn to a rich guy like Kyle?"

Resentful and jealous that Kyle had folks who paved the way for their son's future, complete with a paid in full education, and a no rent agreement in his parents' luxury home. Ben rationalized, "I had to take out school loans, live in a dorm for four years and make extra money in a work study program."

Ben seethed with jealousy when he thought of the financial dichotomy between himself and Kyle. He recalled when Kyle befriended him and shared his ideas on how to make extra money. Ben cringed at how flattered and ready as rain to do whatever Kyle asked of him back then for a monetary reward.

However, now that Ben was out of college, he simply hated Kyle's way of doing things and wished he had parted ways with him when school let out a year ago. "God, what a mess," Ben moaned, "I'm so anxious to get out of town. No more waiting around for Kyle to give the word, no sir, I got my airline ticket online to the Cayman Islands, and I fly out tomorrow afternoon. A few more hours and I'm outta here," Ben mumbled to himself.

Like Eddie, Ben had closed his bank account. Except for the clothes on his back, his flashlight and Kyle's gun which he planned to throw in the ocean right after he picked up his share of the money, Ben dumped everything else he owned in the apartment dumpster. "If Kyle gets in my way," Ben thought, "I just might need the gun. Just to scare him of course. Ben recalled how Kyle shot Sarah and kicked her in the head repeatedly. Now, Sarah's body was at the bottom of Bear Lake along with the bus. "I'm no killer, not yet—I gotta get outta here," Ben moaned.

CHAPTER 12

Tommie Storm Macon paced back and forth on his front porch. He expected HD to show up any minute. His son was never late from school and always called him if he planned to stay over for some event. Tommie had called his son several times but there is no answer.

"Maybe HD told me this morning he was going to be late, and I forgot. I do have lapses of memory, but I almost always remember later," Tommie thought to himself. He did not remember any conversation with HD about being late today. In fact, his son was excited last night—something about college.

Aside from the concern over HD being late Tommie felt good. He had dialysis today and he always felt better afterwards. He sat back in his porch rocker and continued to wait for his son and gaze out over his crops. Tommie Macon's crops lined his driveway all the way to Route 41.

A car turned into the driveway. As the car slowly proceeded towards Tommie's house the car's headlights reflected through the long rows of tall papaya shrubs. Tommie was sure it was

HD and rocked back and forth in his rocker, "He probably missed the bus and caught a ride home with one of his buddies," Tommie thought to himself.

The old man promised himself that he would write things down on the white board his wife put up in the kitchen from now on, and decided not to ask HD why he was late and would pretend that he knew.

When the car arrived at the house and stopped in the turn-around driveway at the front door, blue and white lights blinked and a siren whoop sounded from the vehicle. Tommie's heart took a leap. He breathed heavy and a sharp pain grabbed his chest, he was not prepared to hear bad news. The sight of the deputy's car gave him quite a scare. Deputy Chuck Hillert stepped out of the patrol car and climbed the few steps to the porch.

"Mr. Macon? Tommie Storm Macon?" Deputy Hillert asked. His voice was calm, and he removed his hat out of respect.

"Yes, that's my name, what can I do for you officer," Tommie said, as he rose from his rocker. Tommie shook hands with the young deputy. The officer looked down at a pad then asked Tommie, "Is Daniel Hurricane Dove Macon your son?"

"Yes, he is, we call him HD."

"Has he come home from school yet?"

"No officer, I'm sure he'll be pulling in any moment now, is HD in trouble?" Tommie asked, with a frail shiver in his voice. Officer Hillert hated giving folks bad news, especially parents, "Monroe County school bus number 51 is missing," Hillert said, "your son may be among two other children that we think are still on the bus. We'd like you to come down to the Chief Deputy's office as soon as you can. The parents of the other two children are already there."

Tommie and his wife Mary left immediately, but not before Tommie called his cousin Ronnie Tigertail, "A deputy sheriff 's here at my house Ronnie, he said HD's bus is missing along with HD and two other kids."

Ronnie listened intently, "Okay Tommie, stay calm you never know about these things, maybe the driver took the bus home—I don't know—it doesn't make any sense for the driver to drive off with kids in the bus. Keep us posted on the details—I'll pass this on to everyone. As of now we're on alert," Ronnie assured Tommie.

***

Ronnie quickly called Jamey Johns, a member of the Big Banyan Tribal Council in charge of the Emergency Management portion of their government. In turn, Jamey Johns called Paul Myers, in charge of one of the three broadcasting stations at Big Banyan.

"Don't broadcast anything yet," Ronnie said, "just sit tight until I get back with you. Tommie wouldn't have called me if he didn't think that the bus may have been driven into the glades."

CHAPTER 13

Chief Deputy Lou Slater, together with his three deputies and Detective Morris from Dade County, had been up all night. They had raided a house and nabbed six kidnappers who were wanted for human trafficking. They rescued 20 girls, ages 11 to 18, who were found tied up and sitting on mattresses strewn on the floor of a back room. Work-wise, it had been a good night and Slater was now off duty.

He leaned his elbow on his desk and rubbed his blood shot eyes with both hands. He wished all the noise around him would just stop. Then he could doze off as he waited for the four men and two women that Slater had arrested to be booked and printed.

Slater was anxious to go home and get some sleep, but he had to attend to the parents that had been waiting to see him since ten o'clock last night. So, he tried to make himself presentable and splashed some water on his face and combed his hair. The memo on his desk updated him as to why the parents were so vigilant, having spent all night at the sheriff's office.

The deputies had acquired all the information Slater needed. It included the Amber Alert which went into effect at 6pm last night. They recorded names of the parents, their children and their ages, the ID number of the bus, name of the driver, and her employee background information.

Chief Deputy Slater was tired and not clear-headed enough to begin the missing persons and bus case. He reluctantly washed his face and brushed his teeth, put on a clean shirt, and combed his hair again. The private bath and cot in his office was invaluable. He put on his *this is serious* face then called the families into his office.

It has always been a rare occurrence for any of the tribal people to appear in his office as they had their own Police Department within the Seminole Reservations. In instances where tribal people were involved with off reservation situations, the two law enforcement agencies often worked together. Slater respected the reservation authorities for their efficiency, especially when it came to the Everglades.

Deputy Rudy Pepper escorted the parents into Slater's office, "Good morning, everyone I'm sorry to have kept you waiting so long. I'm Chief Deputy Lou Slater."

After everyone was seated the deputy read a summary of what had been done so far to find their missing children. Ms. Millie Weller, mother to thirteen-year-old Jack, and Mrs. Ellie Culpepper, mother to eight-year-old Billie, cried off and on throughout the night. Their eyes were puffy, and their faces were blotched red. Billie's father, William Culpepper, sat slumped over and weary as he comforted his wife throughout the night. Everyone took a seat except Mr. and Mrs. Macon, who remained standing, their faces grim.

Chief Deputy Slater launched into a speech. "First of all, we are extremely concerned for the wellbeing of the bus driver and your children. The Amber Alert was initiated at 6:00 pm last night and will continue to be broadcast on the news until the children and bus driver are found. We also have witnesses who say they saw the bus yesterday afternoon parked along the side of the road at the intersection of Route 41 and

Flamingo Road. In addition, another vehicle had been seen parked near the bus across from the Tamiami Gas & Shop. According to our eyewitness, a dark green jeep was parked in front of the bus which appeared to have a flat tire. Sometime later the bus disappeared but the jeep was still along the side of the road with a white cloth hanging in one of the jeep windows. It's possible the driver of the jeep had gone for help. By the time our witness left for the night at 11pm both vehicles were gone."

Slater nodded to Mr. and Mrs. Macon as they got up to leave. He hoped Tommie Storm Macon, whose son was one of the Seminole Indian students at the high school, and was among the missing children, would not take matters into his own hands. Slater concluded his report, "We've been out looking for your children for five hours and will continue to do so until everyone is found."

But that was a lie as Slater hadn't assigned anyone to the case yet. Slater walked the remaining parents outside to their cars, "I promise you, that this will be over in no time and that the kids will be found and back home with you safe and sound."

After the parents left, Slater called Deputy Pepper to his office. "Rudy, I want you to get down to the intersection of Route 41 and Flamingo Road. Look for tire tracts and anything else that might have been left behind by that bus and jeep. Send a car all the way down to the end of Flamingo Road and stop at all side roads along the way. A bus is a mighty big vehicle to hide – work your way to Flamingo, past the Visitor Center all the way to the deserted ghost town six miles beyond the Visitor Center. Stop at the Marina, ask if anyone has noticed any recent activity down there. Check out the old Visitor Center for any broken windows, stuff like that, you know the drill."

**

Deputy Pepper was up for detective, and he'd been running high on adrenaline. But now, he was beat, what with the big take down of the human traffickers and rescued missing girls. It had been a successful operation, and he was a very happy man. Now he had another crisis on his plate. "Sir, it just seems that there's always something else. That's the way it is though. Seems like when there's someone crying, there's always someone laughing—the ying and yang of life."

"That's one way of looking at it," Slater said wearily, "the human trafficking case is over, so let's get cracking on the missing children and bus!"

Deputy Pepper smiled as he left Slater's office happy that there was one more check next to his name as the job well done. However, like Chief Deputy Slater he too did an all-nighter. He too was involved in the take-down of the human traffickers and while he still felt the excitement of it all, he needed to get home and get some shut eye.

***

For Chief Deputy Slater, however, work never ends. Today, his work had weighed him down and just as he was about to leave his office, FBI Agent George Russell walked in and flashed his badge at him. "I'm here about the bank robbery," Agent Russell said.

"Okay, come on in," Slater said, a weary edge to his voice, "I thought the FBI had the robbery under control."

"After considerable examination of the point of entry to the vault, that being the vault floor, by way of the bank's basement and accessed by way of a hole in an adjoining wall to a vacant building, I suspect the robbery to be an inside job, and the bank President agrees. I'm convinced of it. There are a lot of details that only an employee could know, I've got the names of all the employees and other info, like addresses, phone numbers, license plates, that sort of thing. I need you to help me run this information and see if anything comes up."

Slater raised an eyebrow and sighed, "Tell you what, I'll have Deputy Danner give you a hand with that, we're on overload and I've got to be somewhere else right about now.

"Jimmy!" Slater yelled out, "give Agent Russell here whatever he needs. He's working the bank robbery. "Yes sir," Deputy Danner said.

Slater picked up his hat and briefcase and headed for the door. He hoped he wouldn't fall asleep on the way home.

***

Before Deputy Danner could help agent Russell, he had to finish taking a statement from Bob Brotelle, the eyewitness from the Tamiami Gas & Shop who saw the school bus pulled over across the highway behind the green jeep.

"Aside from seeing the two vehicles, Bob, you say you also recall that when you left that night both vehicles were gone. By chance did you see the license plate of the jeep or the number on the bus?"

"Actually, I saw both," Bob said, "the jeep was easy to remember because it spelled out KUL-GUY6 and 51 was clearly written on the side of the bus."

"Did you see anyone?" Deputy Danner asked. Bob shook his head, "No sir, I don't recall seeing anybody." Danner shook hands with Bob Brotelle, "Thanks for the information.

Here's my card if you remember anything else give me a call."

"Will do sir," Bob said, "happy to oblige."

Like Slater, Deputy Danner was exhausted too, from the previous night's take down and looked to one of the day shift officers to do the follow-up that the FBI Agent needed. Danner briefed the day shift deputy on Russell's case, handed him the bank's paperwork and headed home to get some much-needed sleep.

***

Meanwhile, Mary and Tommie Storm Macon left the Chief Deputy's office in a hurry. They drove by the Tamiami Gas & Shop where the bus was last seen and turned onto Flamingo Road. Tommie drove slowly, as Mary scanned all along the edge of the sandy shoulder towards the weeds, "Over there," Mary said, "I see large tire tracks and what looks to be a lot of footprints."

Tommy pulled over to the side of the road and got out of his truck to examine the tracks,

"The tire tracks are clear for sure. Large tire tread marks along with a lot of footprints and a place that looks like several sets of footprints well defined."

"Someone or something was shot and fell to the ground. Mary, all the evidence of a struggle is imprinted in the sand. I followed the bus's tread marks. They disappeared at the edge of the road."

Tommie found a patch of something reddish brown—and a bullet shell casing. He pulled out his cell phone and took pictures of the tire tracks, the brown stain in the sand, the shell casing, and footprints.

"Which direction did the bus go from here?"

"The bus would be easy to hide if it was taken into the glades," Mary said.

Tommie looked north at the intersection of Route 41 and Flamingo Road and then he looked down Flamingo Road. It had been 18 hours since the bus was reported missing. Tommie knew every side road and trail of the glades like the back of his hand. He knew where the nearest lake was and especially the Wilderness Waterway.

Tommie was too ill to look for his son. Kidney disease had kept him from working the papaya fields for the past year. It also made his heart condition a ticking time bomb. "I better call Ronnie."

CHAPTER 14

The night before anyone knew the children were missing, frightened, eight-year-old Billy panicked in the dark. He'd never spent time outdoors past dark, not without his parents. He was so relieved when HD lit the fires but still wanted to go home and be with his mother and dad. He wanted to sleep in his own bed and not on a dirty trail of crushed shells and limestone. When the night sounds cranked up Billy started to cry.

Hoot owls hooted lone cries, things buzzed by his head and flicked his ears as they flew by.

"Something is crawling in my hair and on my face, something is in my shirt and it's running up my back!" A bug with a turned-up tail skittered passed Billy. He smacked his tear-stained face and jumped up and down.

Billy wanted to run away but there was nowhere to go except into the pitch-black glades. A bobcat screeched in the distance and Billy screamed back. Jack jumped up and brushed the bugs off Billy. He tried to calm the little boy even though his own arms were covered with mosquitoes. "Stay close to the fire, and pull the smoke towards you like this," HD said as he motioned with his arms and hands, fanning smoke to himself, "and cover your mouth, mosquitoes are attracted to your breath."

Sarah woke when she heard Billy scream, and mumbled, "Bring him over here."

Jack carried Billy, now hysterical, to Sarah and sat him down next to her. She reached out and took his hand in hers.

"Brush the bugs away Billy, brush them away, don't smack them, that's it, just brush them away."

"Now get as close to the fire as you can," Jack said, "and pull the smoke to you like HD's doing. Look at HD, see how he's doing it? Bugs don't like smoke."

Billy calmed down, to the sound of Sarah's weak voice and Jack's encouragement.

***

Meanwhile, HD tended the other two campfires in the middle of the trail. The fires were the best defense against the big cats and snakes; and the smoke helped to keep the bugs at bay. But nothing was perfect, to tend the fires and keep a look out for the nocturnal predators may not be enough to stay awake all night.

***

Billy finally fell asleep in Sarah's good arm. "HD," she whispered, "take him and lay him somewhere else, I can't hold him any longer." HD took Billy in his arms and laid him as close to the fire as he could.

***

Jack sat by the fire cross legged, his back to the darkness. Sweat glistened on his face in the fire light. He held a fern with a long stem, and swatted his back and waved it around to shoo away the hungry mosquitoes.

"Look at 'em all," Jack exclaimed, "never seen such big bugs! So far, I count fifteen scorpions, must be a hundred crickets, the moths are too many to count, and those other bugs— coming into the fire light, I don't know their names."

Jack stayed awake as long as he could, but the hoot owl's lonely calls eventually lulled him to sleep despite the intermittent, low growls and high-pitched screams of a Bobcat from the black void of the glades at night.

***

Unbeknownst to Sarah, HD kept vigil. He watched over her, Billy, and Jack as they slept and carefully maintained the three fires. Sarah moaned in her sleep. HD felt her forehead. Her glistened face burned with fever—her blouse, stained deep red was wet and oozed blood.

Every now and then HD heard a long swish pass by them on both sides of the trail. Whatever it was, stopped and started, stopped and started. He looked up towards the trees. He feared one of them might be swallowed up by a python that lounged on a branch as though it had a front row seat to a meal below. He imagined the python easing its way down from a branch, it could be on them in a heartbeat. So, throughout the night HD walked the edge of the trail and waved a torch above his head to ward off any man-eating snakes that might be high in the branches. On occasion, he sat by the fire to ward off night crawlers that were drawn to the flames.

The crack of lightening, spit crushed shells as it hit the trail a few feet away from the campsite and jolted HD awake. He was unaware that he had dozed off. He hoped it was for only a few seconds. The smell of ozone and rain filled the early morning dawn, and a down pour extinguished the fires. HD put his face to the rain and drank the cool fresh rainwater. Awakened by the lightning strike and sudden downpour, everyone followed suit. The rain beat down on them. The cool downpour washed away yesterday's sweat and dirt. It cleansed their skin, hair, and clothes.

****

Despite the pain, I managed to sit up. I opened my blouse enough, such that the cool rain would cleanse the excruciatingly painful wound. The pelting rain showed no mercy, and I felt as though I would pass out. Nonetheless, the downpour provided a refreshing reprieve from the grit and sweat of the night and cooled my feverish body—but not for long.

The fever returned with a vengeance; my chest wound burned with infection. I was sure I could go no further. I glanced over at the lake. A splash caught my attention. Two young alligators slipped in and out of the water where Jack and Billy had fished yesterday. It gave me a dread feeling to think the gators could have dragged one or both boys into the lake. I couldn't believe our luck.

We had nothing to defend ourselves, yet we'd made it through the night with just the clothes on our backs. If I could just get to my cell phone –but I know that everything is at the bottom of the Lake; cell phones, first aid kit and the kids' back packs. I also know I'm running out of strength. I laid back down on the crusty path, and …

****

Billy and Jack stood a safe distance from the lake, fascinated by the two young gators.

Reptiles they had only seen in pictures and whose carnivorous reputation was the stuff of nightmares. The boys knew well the horror stories of how a gator could steal away a toddler when a young mother took her eyes off her child.

The boys were wide awake after a night's sleep by the campfire, they were alert, refreshed, and drenched by the downpour. HD approached Sarah and sat down next to her.

****

I came to and opened my eyes when HD touched me lightly on my arm. I looked up at a tall teen smiling down at me. I smiled a pitiful grimace back at him, and said, "What does HD stand for?" He looked thoughtful for a moment then said, "Storm Dove."

"But your initial is an H not an S."

"There's no word in my native language that translates to hurricane, only storm. The H is for the Miccosukee word, it spells out phonetically as *hota-lite-soos-kit* first letter being H. My father's name is the same, Storm, but meaning hurricane. My parents say I was born on the night of a hurricane, so they call me by the English word, hurricane, instead of storm."

"What about the D," I asked as I tried to distract myself from a sudden chill and tremor.

"That's from my mother. D is for Dove, she told me that when I was born, I didn't cry I just opened my eyes and breathed quiet like, so they named me Hurricane Dove," HD replied.

I looked at HD and repeated his name several times, "Can you get us outta here—Hurricane Dove?"

"I think so, can you walk?"

"Yes, but I will slow you down. This wound is infected, I have a lot of pain, there is no guarantee I can stay conscious, let alone trudge through these glades. I'm weak, dizzy and my head throbs. Go for help and come back for me, I spent a couple years in the military, I am confident I can take care of myself for a few hours."

"No, it's too dangerous, we must move and keep moving 'till we get to the old Flamingo campground. It's a deserted campground, some refer to it as a ghost town now, but they have fresh water and, from the campground, it's an easy walk to the Flamingo Visitor Center and Marina. You'll be safe at the ghost-town. I can leave you there and go to the Marina for help. There's a phone in the office. If we are lucky, a few fishermen may be docked there."

"What if those guys come back?"

"I'll see them before they see us," HD said, an edge to his voice.

"How long do you think it will take us to get to the ghost-town?"

"We have about a six-mile hike to the ghost-town, we can get there before dark. From there, I'd jog another six miles to the Visitor Center and Marina—if I go alone. If we all could move like trail runners, we'd be at Flamingo in a few hours, but the four of us traveling through the glades and you being wounded will take us longer. We should be going now. It's important we get to Flamingo before dark."

CHAPTER 15

Back in Florida City, Ronnie Tigertail slowly
drove through 600 acres of citrus and monitored
the irrigation system's giant sprinklers as they
spewed huge cascades of water over the vast
rows of orange and lemon trees. His phone
buzzed, "Hello?"

"It's me, Tommie. Yesterday, I found shell
casings and bloodstains not to mention the bus
tracks and footprints in the sand at the
intersection of Route 41 and Flamingo Road.
I'm sure the downpour this morning has washed
it all away. Can you get some people south of
Big Banyan from the Wilderness Waterway
down to Flamingo? I think the Chief Deputy
hasn't sent anyone down Flamingo Road yet. I
suspect that someone is hurt. There's no sign of
the school bus on the highways south to the
Keys and I have a hunch the bus is somewhere
in the glades."

"Tommie, if they were taken into the glades,
we'll find them, I promise."

Within two hours, Ronnie Tigertail recruited
a handful of men; hunters and fishermen who
had grown up in the glades and who knew the

territory from Big Banyan Reservation, south sixty-eight miles to Flamingo, east to Tamiami and west to the outer islands.

While the park service had maps of all the trails, lakes, waterways and campsites, the Seminole people of Big Banyan had their own trails, forged several hundred years earlier by their ancestors, hidden and unknown to park rangers, hikers, and tourists.

Shortly after Ronnie's call, trackers, better known as trail runners, went into action. They drove an ATV, through the glades. They stayed on the park's trails that lead to a public campsite and pulled into the campsite. They parked the ATV in the campsite's parking lot. From there, the trail runners moved quickly on foot and within minutes they veered off the trail and disappeared into the glades. On an uncharted trail, the trackers traveled south towards the Wilderness Waterway. It's been twenty-four hours since the children and bus were last seen.

The trail runners traveled light; a rifle, a long knife, and a bottle of water for each of them, lots of bug repellant and flashlights, they moved through the glades at a jog alternating with a fast-moving walk. They covered three to five miles an hour and by dawn they were only four miles north of the Wilderness Waterway when the torrential twenty-minute downpour forced them to take cover.

Once the storm subsided, the trackers crossed over the Waterway and headed for the intersection of Bear Lake Road and Bear Lake Trail. Instead of going forward towards Bear Lake Road, they turned towards the trail that led to the lake. It wasn't long before they came across the remains of three campfires.

Thin tendrils of smoke floated out of the soggy mound of blackened ash and limbs of the first campfire. Next to the remains of the second campfire, twigs had been laid out on the ground in the form of two letters—H.D.

At the third campfire sight, the one closest to the lake, they found a fish head and two tree-branch fishing poles. A gator slithered into burnt yellowish brown brackish water. A color caused by the tannin of decomposing bark and plants. When the water rippled away from the splash, orange paint of a bus, and white trim around windows blurred into view. Ronnie Tigertail had instructed them before they headed out,

"Don't tamper with anything, just observe and report back to us." The runners knew better than to try to retrieve bodies from the bus, and to jump into the brackish lake would be unwise as it was home to at least two alligators if not more.

Minutes later, Ronnie received a call from the trail runners who found the bus, he called Paul Bowman, the Big Banyan Police Chief. "Better for Slater to hear this from you, Paul, than us. We don't need any suspicion coming our way," Ronnie recommended to Bowman.

"Tommie Storm Macon's son was on the bus when it disappeared," Paul Bowman said, "that should be reason enough as to why we're interested."

"They'll want to talk to the trail runners," Bowman said.

"Okay, but they're tracking the kids as we speak, I'll tell them where the bus is, that ought to keep them busy for a while, and also about the footprints, tire tracks, shell casing and blood along the side of the road where the bus was last seen."

Ronnie hung up and called Tommie. "The bus was dumped in Bear Lake. While the trail runners don't know if anyone is in the bus there is evidence that the kids could be alive. HD left his initials spelled out in twigs and we found a fish head and two tree-branch fishing poles at the lake."

"We'll find them Tommie, don't you worry. HD knows his way around the glades. Besides, the lead trail runner, Denis Watergrass, who is still hunting deer, wild boar, pythons and other wild game in the everglades, hunted alongside you and HD many times. You all went hunting almost every weekend during the winter months."

"Hunters rarely hunt during the summer, wet season," Tommie said before he hung up the phone.

"Yea, I know," Ronnie said to himself as he tried to remain positive.

Meanwhile, Denis and the other trail runners examined the remains of the campfires they think HD built. They checked out the fishing poles and the fish heads found at the lake's edge. Denis called Ronnie, who asked, "Which way did they go?"

"All the signs point to a westward move around the lake. Why HD chose to go through the glades, and not just come up Bear Lake Road to Flamingo, didn't make sense. The kids would've been picked up by now. And I wonder why the bus was dumped in the lake."

"Don't know, Ronnie, we can only follow the trail through the glades."

Denis hung up and announced to his trackers, "Just to be sure the kids are not walking up Flamingo Road. You two guys go to the end of Bear Lake Road. See if they are somewhere stranded out there. If they made it to Flamingo Road, the children would surely be picked up. Perhaps it's a good thing that there are no signs of the kids."

Denis called Ronnie again, "Just found another sign; an H carved in a cypress tree at the edge of the campfire, I think we need to track the kids into the glades, why else would HD leave such an obvious sign?"

"I agree, and I'll wait until I hear from you before I call Slater, give you a chance to find the kids alive. It will go better for everyone that way. Telling Tommie is enough for now, it's important for HD's dad to know that your findings point to the fact that HD is still alive and moving westward."

Denis and the trackers stepped into the steamy humid glades and became invisible within seconds. They found the old Bear Lake Trail around the west end of the lake. It was overgrown and barely visible as no one had traveled the trail in years.

The trail would have been lost forever had it not been made with the white limestone and shells dug out of the man-made waterways. The indigenous gravel was specifically used to blaze trails throughout the glades for hikers. Denis was six hours behind HD.

CHAPTER 16

HD stood tall at six-feet-two inches, broad shouldered and strong well-muscled legs. He regularly hunted in the everglades alongside experienced hunters and trail runners of the Big Banyan Reservation, which contributed considerably towards his strength and stamina. HD's complexion bore a deep copper tan from the long hours he worked in his father's papaya fields and hours spent hunting in the glades.

It was fortuitous that Billy, Jack, and Sarah had HD with them. He had rescued them from the horrendous nightmare that had beset them, and now guided them through the glades. Sarah was having blackouts and was unable to walk so HD carried her on his back. He looked to Jack and said, "Keep Billy close, by your side, carry him if you must."

***

Jack, a boney kid, two heads shorter than HD and all arms and legs, took Billy's hand and kept stride with HD whom he had quickly grown to admire, such that when Billy tired out and wanted to stop and rest, Jack just picked him up and carried Billy piggy-back style the way HD carried Sarah and walked until HD was ready to stop and rest.

Aside from being hard to find, the trail was soaked and alive with wetland creatures which up until now were hidden amongst the brush in the trail. They moved quickly and hoped there'd be no confrontations with the glade's snakes, feral hogs, alligators, bobcats, and panthers. It was bad enough to deal with the sweltering summer heat and biting bugs that came at them constantly.

The walk around the lake was too close to the densely tangled mangroves for HD's liking. Carrying Sarah piggy-back, he moved as quietly and as quickly as possible. The ground gradually became less soggy the further away from the lake they hiked. Finally, they made it to the hammocks.

The trail of limestone and crushed shells had gradually transformed from a wetland path to a long stretch of dry ground surrounded by an expanse of parched, golden-brown, waist high river grass. Fortunately, the hammock had at least a good three hundred yards to the tree line on either side of the trail, however, it was barely visible through the high river grass. Dead center and in the distance, HD saw a small stand of hardwoods.

The crunch of limestone and shells assured HD that they were on the trail headed into the hardwoods. Anything could happen between now and the time it took to get to the hardwoods. The waist high river grass was home to feral hogs, anacondas, rattlers and pythons.

Hunters who often lodged high in the trees had reported sightings of pythons and anacondas, whose thick sinuous bodies, swollen with a recent feast, could be seen slithering through the river grass, across the hammocks, from one end to the other.

As they prepared to walk another hour or so, HD hoped the growling of a wild hog up ahead would fade away. Suddenly, Jack noticed that HD started clapping his hands, "Why are you clapping your hands?"

"Step careful in my footsteps behind me Jack, when I stop you stop, okay?" HD took careful steps and stopped every now and then to clap his hands. In response, the grasses ahead of him moved.

"What was that?"

"A startled rattle snake, over there, hidden in the grasses, they don't like loud noises, it's slithering away now. So far, we haven't run into any pythons or anacondas."

As the small group of weary travelers continued their journey forward, the high keening wail of the feral hog sounded closer and closer, and it no longer sounded like a growl. HD wondered, "What are the chances it's something that's caught our scent and is hunting us."

"What is that?" Jack asked alarmed at the screeching sounds.

"Sounds like a feral hog, hope it isn't a male," HD replied.

That's the last thing HD wanted to deal with—wild hog attacks were vicious. He reached down to touch his knife which was now secured to his belt. Nothing more was said about the hog. HD figured there was no sense in scaring anyone unless and until they come upon one. The hog screamed out several more times, each scream sounded closer than the last.

Gradually, the river grass gave way to a sparse scrubby ground cover around the limestone trail. The hardwoods were clearly visible and about a quarter mile away. HD was relieved at the opening in the high grass. About one hundred feet ahead he could see something on the right side of the trail.

A large dark green object lay half in and half out of their path. Another loud scream stopped HD in his tracks. Up ahead the screams came from whatever was on the trail, and it was no hog. "Something's wrong," HD said as he moved forward a few steps at a time. All the while his eyes focused on the large green thing on the trail. The hog screamed out again, this time its cry stopped in mid-scream.

"I've heard many stories of giant snakes in the glades from some of my hunting friends. I thought I'd seen them all, but just ahead, Jack, on the trail, wound up like a giant spring, is a dark green anaconda and it's wrapped around a feral hog that was screaming up until a few minutes ago."

114

"Its mouth is wide open, HD, and it's got a hold of the hog in the neck."

"Yea, can't see its teeth because they're inverted, sharp and locked into the hog's neck It's coiled so tight around the hog that it must have squeezed the life out of it." With Sarah on his back, HD turned to Jack,

"Stay close behind me, stay quiet," he whispered. Jack and Billy stared horrified at the sight of the massive green anaconda wrapped around the hog, its teeth anchored in its' neck. Terrified, they quietly walked a wide circle around the massive snake, whose eyes follow them as if to size them up for its next meal. As soon as Billy and Jack got passed the snake HD signaled Jack to follow him, and he broke into a steady jog.

"The trail's a straight shot through the hammock, Jack, and we can stop and rest at the clump of hardwoods up ahead. I sure hope there's nothing waiting for us when we get there, I can only hope." Stoically, Jack followed behind HD, as he chastised himself, "Don't you dare cry."

When they arrived at the hardwoods, HD gently placed Sarah in the shade of a large palm tree. She was unconscious and burned with fever. "How much farther to Flamingo?" Jack asked as Billy slid off his back.

"Two miles, HD said, "we've moved quicker than I thought we could and I'm sure we'll get there before dark."

"Sarah needs a doctor," Jack said fearfully.

"I know, wish we could do more for her, Jack." HD replied.

"Can you at least get the bullet out of her, HD? You know, like they do in the cowboy movies?"

"I think the bullet passed through her Jack, the back of her shirt is bloody. I thought about cauterizing the wound, but I'm not sure it's the right thing to do at this time, what with all the infection oozing out of it." Billy sat next to Sarah, and patted her hand, "Please don't die Miss Sarah, please don't die."

"Nobody's dying today, Billy. Come on we've rested long enough, let's get out of here," HD ordered, "next stop's the Flamingo campgrounds."

Once again, Jack and HD hoisted Sarah and Billy onto their backs and set out on a brisk walk. The sun was in the western sky when the weary troupe arrived at the deserted Flamingo campgrounds. The sound of waves crashed into the shore and a cool ocean breeze greeted them. Any juice from HD's crushed leaves that gave relief from the flying insects had long faded away. Their faces, necks and arms were blotched with quarter size welts from bug bites, and their skin was hot with sunburn.

An empty deserted grocery store leaned north at the entrance to the empty campground. The southern end of the old grocery building was blown away by hurricanes. On the weathered side of the dilapidated old building was a freshwater faucet that coughed, and spit rust colored water for a few seconds before the water ran clear.

The kids took turns at the spigot drinking and splashing water over themselves. HD had laid Sarah atop a concrete picnic table. She was too weak to sit up. HD removed his shirt and rinsed it under the spigot. He soaked it through until it was dripping wet. Then, he took it to Sarah and wrung out the water from the shirt over Sarah's parched face and lips.

"Where are we, HD?"

"We're at the Flamingo campgrounds about six miles from the Marina. These campgrounds have been deserted for years. We must get to the Marina. If I go alone, I can get there before dark. If we all go together, it will take longer, there are no streetlights this far from the Visitor Center, we would be walking in the dark before we get there. We would have to grope our way down the asphalt road. Without light it's too dangerous."

Sarah pleaded, "Don't leave us here, I can't protect them."

"Stay here at the ghost town and rest. If I go alone," HD argued, "I'd be at the Marina an hour after dark, I'll get into the Marina and use their phone to call for help."

"We made it through an entire night already," Sarah insisted, "we can handle one more hour."

"How come there's nobody here, HD," Billy asked, "this is a great spot!"

"Hurricanes wiped out the sheltered campground areas. The Florida Park Service got tired of rebuilding it only to have another hurricane blow it to smithereens again. My father said that the glades grew clear up to the Florida Bay. To develop the campground the state cleared it all out to make way for rows and rows of concrete pads and electrical hook-ups for the camper's RVs and tents. Then the hurricanes came, one right after another and devastated this place. The National Park people abandoned the area and the glades reclaimed it. Only things left are a few concrete picnic tables—and this," HD turned toward the Florida Bay. The pristine shoreline was littered with beautiful shells.

The exhaustion of the day had set in, and HD was too tired to appreciate the beauty of it all. The night came quicker than HD anticipated, so he decided to stay at the campground with Sarah and the boys. As the dark of night crept over the Bay of Florida, Jack, Billy and Sarah spread out on the concrete slabs of the picnic tables and were asleep in minutes. HD was the last to fall asleep.

The ocean breezes blew steadily and strong, and scattered mosquitoes and other night flyers away from the weary travelers as they slept.

CHAPTER 17

When Denis arrived at the Flamingo campgrounds, he was relieved to find HD, two children and a woman asleep on the picnic tables. He touched HD on the shoulder and whispered, "Hey man wake up, it's me, Denis." HD jolted up and jumped off the table. He backed away from Denis and pulled his knife.

"Take it easy, HD, it's me, Denis. We tracked you from the Big Spring Campground north of the Waterway. We've been looking for you for hours!"

HD, looked past the glare of a wide face flashlight, "Denis? Denis Watergrass?"

"Yea, man, take it easy, we're sure glad we found you; your folks are worried sick." HD sighed, and reached out to shake Denis's hand and whispered, "Let's talk over here, I don't want to wake them just yet."

HD led the trail runners to the rundown grocery building and told them everything that happened from the time the bus picked him up from school yesterday afternoon up until now. He recounted the nightmare of the previous day from the time Sarah had stopped at the stop light and the three guys with a green jeep forced their way into the bus at gunpoint, to their arrival at the picnic tables. HD left nothing out, and for the first time since the hijacking somehow the telling of his experience broke HD down and he wept as he spoke. "It was bad enough with the shootout at school, which I still have nightmares about, then to be hijacked with two kids and a wounded bus driver. I'm afraid she'll die if we don't get help soon, not to mention the fear of getting attacked and eaten by the biggest predators in the glades or losing one of the younger boys."

Denis listened quietly, as HD told him what happened and how they wound up on the shores of Florida Bay in the rundown campground. HD let it all out. Then his tears turned to anger towards those guys who did this to them. "I have never wanted to kill anyone, ever, but those men—they tried to kill us and nearly killed Ms. Sarah. I'm ready to cut their throats and hang 'em out to dry Denis." HD wiped humiliating tears from his face.

"Take it easy HD, it's over now. We're here to get you home." Denis put his arm around HD to calm him and thought to himself what a harrowing story of a near death experience for all of them. Especially Sarah Miller, who lay asleep or was unconscious on one of the stone tables desperately in need of a doctor.

"At first, I thought we could make it as far as the Marina, HD said, "but I carried Miss Sarah most of the way and I was too exhausted, man, I had to rest, we all did. If the kidnappers are still hanging around the Visitor Center, we won't be seen if we continue tonight. I planned to call the police at the Marina. But now that you're here we can call now."

Denis looked back and forth at the trail runners, and they all shook their heads no, "Our phones ran out of charge an hour ago, but we do have plenty of flashlights so we can all go to the Marina together. Let me introduce these guys to you HD, you know Mark Morris, and this is Joel and Chris Bowman, the Chief's kids." HD reached out and shook hands with them, "Thanks for coming."

"We'll take it from here HD, everything is gonna be fine now," Joel reassured him.

"We should be going before it gets much later. We haven't eaten since Billy and Jack caught a couple of rainbow bass at Bear Lake last night." HD said.

"Yea, we found the fish head, the fishing poles, nice job making them by the way, and your initials, good work HD. When this is over you should get a medal or something," Chris said.

HD woke Billy and Jack and introduced them to the trail runners. Sarah moaned and woke briefly only to pass out. "Let me carry her HD," Denis offered, and together with Joel, HD carefully lifted Sarah onto Denis's back. "I can carry this little guy here," Chris said as he pointed to Billy, "what's your name?"

"Billy," and the eight-year-old wasted no time telling Chris about the fish he and Jack caught, and the huge snake with horrible fangs and the feral hog that it squeezed to death. The more the little boy talked the tighter he held onto Chris.

***

Jack walked alongside Denis and HD, relieved that Chris offered to carry Billy and for the first time in 24 hours, Jack was not afraid. He was so overcome with relief at being rescued, that tears flowed freely down his cheeks, but he didn't care. HD made Jack feel as though he was the high school senior's equal.

Because of the harrowing experience of the past 24 hours, thirteen-year-old Jack had come to know HD, the high school senior who saved their lives and it made Jack feel important with a measure of control over his life. Back home it was just Jack and his mom. For the first time ever, Jack felt like a man, a good man.

***

The midnight trek to the Marina was uneventful and the ocean breezes kept the flying bugs at bay. Together with the trail runners, the 6 mile walk to the Marina seemed to go by faster than the hike through the glades. They arrived at the Marina in two hours. HD immediately noticed lights in the windows of the Visitor Center, just across from the Marina. A white truck, a jeep and another car were parked just outside the building. Denis motioned for everyone to be as quiet as possible as he led the weary group across the wooden pier to the Marina.

HD seethed with anger, "Quick! Get inside the Marina, it's probably those guys who hijacked the bus."

Denis jimmied the lock, and everyone quietly slipped into the all-purpose Canteen. The place was full of bait and tackle amidst rows and rows of packaged snacks, drinks, and a variety of tourist clothes.

Across the street, loud angry voices echoed through the night, glass shattered, and several loud gun shots rang out from the upstairs room. Denis and HD peered out a window that faced the Marina. "I recognize that jeep," HD whispered, "That's the jeep that was pulled over to the side of the road where we got hijacked."

****

I awoke to the sound of gunshots and tried to lift myself up from the floor. I wondered if we were under attack, but I could only cry out in pain and collapsed. A voice said, "Ma'am, take it easy, it's alright we're all safe here, can you understand me?" I nodded and asked, "Who are you, where's HD and the kids?"

"My name is Denis, and we have just arrived at the Marina across the street from the Flamingo Visitor Center. I know you're in a lot of pain, and we're going to take care of you here. Do you think you can recognize any of the vehicles across the street that were near the bus when it was hijacked?"

I covered my mouth to muffle my cries as Denis lifted me up far enough to see out the window, my mouth tasted like blood. "Is that the jeep that was parked along the road when you pulled up to the stoplight the other day, the one HD said had a flat tire?" Denis asked.

I lean against the window, it took a few seconds for me to focus before I could see well enough to recognize the jeep, "I can't make out the color in the dark. I'd have to see the license plate, it's a unique plate, you know, it spells out a word or two."

"Can you stay by the window, and I'll sneak out there and shine the flashlight on the license plate, can you do that?" Denis asked, "by the way, I'm Denis Watergrass."

"Yea, I think so," I said as blood dripped from my mouth, "tell Billy to bring me something to sit on and I should be alright for a bit unless I pass out." Billy ran to the office and returned with a stool. He set it down under the window for Sarah. "Me and Jack will take care of her in case she starts to fall," Billy said.

HD and the four trail runners quietly made their way to the cars and hid behind the jeep. Denis turned the flashlight on the license plate and held it there for thirty seconds. He hoped Sarah could see it. Then under cover of darkness they ran back to the Marina amidst the shots and shouts from above the Visitor Center.

"That's it," I breathed and slid down to the floor, "You don't forget a plate like that, KUL-GUY6." Breathless I asked, "Has anyone called an ambulance yet?" I choked on a mouthful of blood and gasped for air through piercing pain, then nothing.

******

HD groped around in the office in the dark, until he came to a desk. On the desk was a phone, "No dial tone, Denis."

"Maybe the powers been shut off for the season. See if you can find a breaker box, HD."

After poking around the office, a locked desk and file cabinet, HD got restless, "I think we need to keep moving, these guys are killers. They shot Sarah, kicked her in the head repeatedly and dumped the bus in Bear Lake. They thought she was still in the bus," HD's voice tone was grim and threatening, "we were lucky to get out with our lives."

"Take it easy HD, we found the doused fires, and the bus, and we reported to Chief Bowman, our findings, they know we headed south to Flamingo," Denis continued, "you're right though, we need to get moving. Also, if we're here when the authorities come, there's a chance we might get caught in a crossfire. The authorities will figure this out, HD."

"I hope you're right, that there's someone out there looking for us, Denis. The sooner we get out of here the better." Denis grabbed his rifle, "Okay then, let's do this, I'm confident we'll meet up with the authorities before we get to Tamiami Trail."

"Hope the flashlights hold up," Joel said. "It's 30 miles to Tamiami Trail! We'll never make it before morning, not with Billy and Sarah, they'll slow us down, Denis."

"We won't make it before morning with or without Sarah," Denis replied.

*****

I overheard the boys arguing in whispered tones and interrupted them, "I don't want to move anymore."

I realized that I might not make it through the night. I pushed myself up against the wall, "Leave me—and a rifle, I can take care of myself until you get help," I lied as I breathed shallow breaths, "There's plenty of water, probably some first aid stuff on the shelves, a good dose of any antibiotic will help, probably some peroxide. Look around and see what you can find before you leave." Billy looked at me, "I'm staying with you, Miss Sarah," Billy said fearfully.

"You can sit here next to me Billy, don't worry, we'll be fine," I assured him even though I was convinced I'd be dead by morning. I looked up at Denis and said a second time,

"Just leave me a rifle, you know, just in case those idiots make their way over here."

I leaned back against the wall and breathed slowly; my head reeled with dizziness.
HD knelt next to me and wracked several bullets into the chamber of one of the rifles and set it against the wall. "I shouldn't leave you here, Miss Sarah, it's wrong to leave you by yourself."

"I just might not die if you all get out of here and go for help. Denis is right, people are looking for us and you will meet up with them on the way, I know it's just a guess but I'm staking my life on it. Talking is making me dizzy. Now go! I insist."

After HD gave me the loaded rifle and one of the flashlights, he joined the others. I could hear them rummaging around on the shelves. I hoped they were looking for bandages, peroxide, and boxes of antibiotic ointment. Sure enough, HD laid out the first aid supplies next to me along with a six pack of bottled water. He knelt next to me one more time. Before he could say anything, I reached up and touched his face,

"Hurricane Dove," I wheezed, "you did good—now go! I'll be okay. If anyone knows how to use a rifle, it's me. You may not know this, but I held my own in Afghanistan for four years, I'm a good shot," I said between shallow breaths, "remember, stay alert, and stay alive."

CHAPTER 18

With Sarah and Billy safely tucked in at the Marina, the trail runners, HD, and Jack slipped out the back door that led to a small parking lot. Aside from the dim light across the street at the Visitor Center, the night was pitch black. To avoid being detected by the men in the Visitor Center, HD's group walked in the dark until the light from the Visitor Center was no longer visible.

"You know, for all the times I've hunted in the glades," Denis said, "this is the first time I've been here at night, in the rainy season." Denis chuckled as he flipped on a flashlight.

"It's gonna be interesting," Mark whispered, as he shifted his eyes left to right.

Joel, Chris, and Jack took up the rear, their flashlights scanned the glades on either side of Flamingo Road. The cacophonous chatter of sounds coming out of the glades never let up. Fortunately, everyone was thoroughly doused with the trail runner's bug-spray. However, the large hungry flying bugs smacked into them, crawled in their hair and skittered over their clothes. The first python presented itself within an hour of the long walk—the men stopped and waited quietly as it slithered slowly from one side of the road to the other. Denis estimated its length at twenty feet. The center of the snake bulged out, which as far as the men were concerned was a good thing. It appeared to have recently had a meal and an attack on them would be unlikely.

The trail runners took up a pattern of walk/jog, walk/jog, and paced themselves to go as far and as fast as they could. They never let up and moved as quickly as possible without burning out. They dared not stand still for more than a few minutes. The screams of bobcats and the growls of other large predators was just too close to call. At one point, several deer darted across the road with a bobcat close behind, oblivious of the four men who stood stock still twenty feet away.

They targeted their flashlights on the bobcat as it ran after the deer deep into the glades. Then they waited a few minutes in case the bobcats were hunting in pairs and a second bobcat showed itself. Further down the road, they came across something large and unrecognizable in the center of the road. No one knew what it was, until they got close enough to hear the *sh sh sh sh* sound of it.

Sprawled out before them was a red mound comprised of thousands of fire ants persistent in their consumption of some animal, that still moved beneath them. Denis turned and whispered to everyone, "Back up some, we need to get around that mound without disturbing it. No fooling around or trying to poke at it, the ants will attack us, and we don't want anyone of us to wind up like the thing they're eating right now."

"I'll go first," Mark said, "don't shine the flashlights on them, just a quick, quiet walk around, got it?" Everyone nodded yes, and followed Mark around the red mound of carnivorous, fire ants. After everyone was clear of the mound, Jack said, "That's just plain creepy, I'm gonna have nightmares for a month."

For now, everyone walked in silence, lost in their own thoughts. HD wondered what they would run into next. "Here's a story for you," Chris said, "I read somewhere that a big ole anaconda, huge thing, was all curled up around her eggs. Fire ants came up from underneath the snake and ate the snake and all her eggs. Within hours all that was left was scales and bones."

"Scales and bones! That's hard to believe," Jack exclaimed.

"Well, snakes won't move when they're protecting their eggs, see, and the ants swarmed her and ate them all."

Chris boasted, a little pride in his voice for knowing a bit of wilderness trivia. "Did you see the green anaconda eating a feral hog when you got to the hammock?" HD asked. Denis looked back at him, "Yea, we saw it, better the hog than us. Last year a group of us went out from Big Banyan and came across one of those monsters, it attacked one of the guys. Before we killed it, the snake gored him and bit his legs something fierce," Denis recalled.

"I didn't know we had green anacondas in the glades until today," HD said, "lucky it was busy with the hog, or it would have attacked one of us I'm sure of it."

"And I hear their fast, that's what I hear," Jack exclaimed.

"Too bad we can't break into song or think happier thoughts," Mark said with a smirk on his face. "Be serious now," Denis said, "when we approach Bear Lake Road keep your eyes peeled, gators have been seen coming across the road."

"I hate to say it," said Mark, "but it's mating season for the panthers, they come south this time of year, they're nocturnal and—carnivores.

"Thanks for sharing," Denis said, a bit of sarcasm in his voice, "why don't you scare us with another wilderness nightmare."

Remembering what Sarah said before they left the Marina, HD repeated, "Stay alert, stay alive."

"Amen to that!" Mark exclaimed.

The walk in the pitch dark was made worse by the stifling humidity and despite the insect repellant, a variety of biting mosquitoes attacked mercilessly. Every now and then Jack turned around to see if anything was following them. On one such occasion, he noticed green marble sized lights looking back at him.

Sometimes the lights winked out only to reappear again. When the lights got closer, Jack said, "Hey guys, check out the little lights behind us." Everyone turned around.

Denis put his rifle to his shoulder, aimed it up and pulled the trigger. Everyone pointed their flashlights towards the direction of the small marble sized lights, "Geez, look at the size of it," Denis exclaimed.

The flashlights exposed a panther. It growled and bared its teeth. Ready to pounce, head hung low, it stood its ground behind them for a few seconds. Startled by the rifle shot and the blinding flashlights, it turned and receded into the glades. Denis turned to Jack. "Next time you see eyes looking at us, you need to tell us pronto, you understand Jack?" HD warned, "Like Sarah said, stay alert, stay alive!"

"I didn't know it was a panther, honest!" Jack exclaimed terrified.

"It's mating season, if there's one, there's more, all that yowling out there may well happen to be a female in heat," Mark surmised, "like I said, they're carnivores, they eat meat, like deer, hogs, and PEOPLE!" he shouted.

"They don't eat people," HD chided, "they're relatively shy, more afraid of us than we are of them."

"Like I said," Mark insisted, "it's mating season, and anything goes, the males are a bit more aggressive this time of year."

"Knock it off, Mark, enough said about the panthers," HD insisted, "nothing is gonna eat us. Jack, just stay close."

CHAPTER 19

Prior to everyone's arrival at the Marina, and in the middle of the pitch-black night, Kyle had arrived at the Visitor Center.

"This place is creepy at night, deserted, no lights," he said to himself. Kyle sat in his car getting up the courage to run up the metal stairs to the upper room of the Visitor Center. He pulled out his biggest flashlight, got out of the car and turned the flashlight on. His feet struck a hollow clang as he ran up the metal steps.

Suddenly, Kyle's leadership confidence gave way to beads of sweat as he fumbled with the lock. It didn't help that he was dressed in black from head to foot. At the time that he planned to put the money back, it didn't dawn on him that an all-black ensemble to hide his identity, complete with ski mask would be a little warm in the hot humid Florida night.

The lock finally gave way. Kyle entered the dank, hot room, threw off his mask and tore off his long sleeve jacket. The six bags of money lay in a heap where he, Ben and Eddie had tossed them the other day. He grabbed two bags and headed down the steps.

"What are you doing Kyle?"

Ben stood just below Kyle on his way up the steps, having arrived minutes after Kyle climbed the metal stairs. "Oh hey, guys, I was just uh, taking my share."

"We need to split it three ways—evenly" Eddie said, "right Ben?"

"Right."

"Uh, sure, sure, I'm pretty sure all the bags have about the same amount of money in them, heh, heh." Kyle backed up into the upper room and dropped the bags.

While Eddie confronted Kyle, Ben turned on his lantern. A soft light filled the room, "What's with the black outfit, man," Eddie asked. Kyle threw his hands in the air, turned around and said, "I can't do this, I wanna put the money back in the bank, I think they're on to me!" Dumbfounded, Ben and Eddie stared at Kyle. "They brought in the FBI, and they know the heist is an inside job. On top of that, the money is marked, somehow, they can trace it. We can't spend it; we can only hide it or bury it for god knows how long. If we make large deposits or buy anything like a car, and we pay cash, the dealerships and banks look at it as suspicious money and they can nab us."

"I'm not going down for this, not now that the FBI's involved. And another thing," Kyle continued, "the FBI guy at the bank said that every merchant in the nation knows that large conspicuous purchases with large amounts of money are called into the police. They'll make the sale alright, then they'll turn right around and call it in, and/or any deposit over ten thousand dollars is automatically reported to the US Treasury Department. Slightly less than ten thousand could be considered suspicious and recorded on a suspicious activity report better known in the bank world as SAR."

Ben and Eddie looked at their fearless leader as though he had suddenly become a crybaby.

"Hold it right there Kyle, you're going to take your share back to the bank, then what, you rat us out?" Ben said in a threatening voice tone. Ben turned to Eddie, whose face had gone white, and nodded, "What are you thinking Kyle, come on man, I can't believe this—you can leave the country!"

"That's right, what did you expect would happen when you rob a bank, Kyle," Eddie said, a little anger in his voice, "why do you think me and Ben are getting out of Florida, going out of state, out of country, to the Cayman Islands and beyond! Did you think there would be no repercussions, no investigations, no smart cops out there that could figure out a bank robbery?"

"I got my passport," Ben said, "I know Eddie's got his, you wouldn't happen to have your passport on you, would you Kyle?" Ben asked as he reached behind his back and slowly pulled out one of Kyle's guns from his back pocket and held it behind his leg.

Kyle realized the threat Ben posed, "I should kill 'em, then I could say it was all their fault and that I was held at gunpoint," Kyle thought to himself. "I'd never rat you guys out!" Kyle lied, "have I ever let you down? We can live to do a heist another day. But this one is out of our league; don't you see that?"

"Kyle, why can't you leave the country with us, it's the only way," Ben argued, "why in the world do you want to hang around here?"

Kyle and Ben got into a shouting match. Each became more threatening than the other. Eddie took several steps backward. He saw that each of his friends held a handgun behind their backs, "Oh no," Eddie said under his breath, "they're gonna shoot it out."

Kyle fired first, Ben returned fire and missed Kyle. If Kyle and Ben had any experience with guns, they'd have shot each other dead on the first shot, but neither of them could claim experience with guns. The shots zinged over their heads or into the walls. Ben finally shot true and hit Kyle in the head, but not until Kyle's shot spewed window glass all over the street below. The room was silent. Ben stood over Kyle and looked down at him, "He's dead Eddie. He didn't have a passport with him anyway."

Ben was void of remorse for killing Kyle. Eddie had curled up in a corner far from the shoot-out, his hands over his ears. "Come on Eddie, help me split the money 50/50 and get the hell outta here."

They tied up the six canvas bags and carried them down to the vehicles two at a time.

144

"Ben, what should we do with Kyle's body, we can't leave it here?"

"Help me bring him downstairs, and we'll put him in his car."

Ben and Eddie carried Kyle's body downstairs and set him up in the driver's seat of his jeep. Suddenly from across the street a Johnny Cash country and western tune blared out of the Marina's bull horn speakers. Eddie and Ben looked at each other and quickly put out the lantern.

"Somebody's over there," Eddie whispered.

"Yea," Ben said, "and I bet they didn't mean to turn on those lights or blare music through a bull horn across the Florida Bay to Cuba. Now who could that be? Maybe—a bus driver. Maybe, Kyle didn't kill her after all, maybe she got away, and is sitting over there calling the sheriff right about now," Ben said through gritted teeth, "why am I not surprised?"

"Look I don't care who's over there, I'm taking my share and I'm outta here Ben," Eddie said.

Ben and Eddie continue to load their vehicles with the lights of the Marina across the street.

Suddenly the music stopped in mid-tune, and the lights went out. The Marina was dark and silent.

"Okay Eddie, you can go if you want, I'm gonna find out who's hiding over there," Ben decided.

"Ben, leave it, we have to get out of here—now."

"Nope, Eddie, I am on a roll. No more listening to anyone, I am my own man, and I have made some serious decisions tonight. You should be thanking me Eddie for having Kyle's other gun, the one he used to shoot the bus driver, or else he would have killed us. Now you hang tight Eddie, I'll be right back."

Ben slowly walked toward the Marina. He reached for the pistol tucked in his jeans and traced the outline of it with his hand. Eddie sat in his truck ready to go, "You got five minutes, Ben, five minutes, then I am outta here."

CHAPTER 20

I positioned the flashlight such that I could see and rummage through the things the boys laid out for me; first aid kit, medicines, water, aspirin, and bandages. I wanted to clean the wound, even though it would hurt like hell. At least it would slow the infection from getting worse, maybe be a reprieve from the fever too.

I unwrapped a package of bandages and opened several tubes of antibiotic. The gunshot wound oozed only when I touched it, I didn't know if that was a good thing or not. I swallowed a handful of aspirin, and wondered what HD used to ease the pain back at the lake. I made a mental note to ask him when this was all over, if I—live long enough that is.

I peeled off my shirt and slathered on several tubes of antibiotic ointment then placed a square bandage over the wound. I taped several smaller bandages with sticky edges onto the larger dressing to hold it in place. Then I applauded myself for not screaming.

I shined the flashlight around the store, until I caught sight of some tourist t-shirts. I knew that at this point I risked hurting myself worse if

I moved and certainly, I'd pass out again. I whispered to Billy who was asleep next to me, "Billy, wake up, I need you to grab some t-shirts off the clothes rack and bring them to me."

Billy brought me a handful of shirts. I never dreamed I'd be in so much pain as I struggled to get into one of them. I've never been so exhausted in my life including the time I spent in Afghanistan. I looked down at Billy, who had curled up next to me and fallen back to sleep. I positioned myself in a sitting position against a wall under the window that faced the Visitor Center. I set the loaded rifle across my legs.

I must have blacked out. When I came to Billy was awake and softly shaking me. "Hey Billy, I whispered.

"Hey Miss Sarah, how're feeling?" the little boy asked.

"Been better. I'm sure we're going to get through this very soon."

But I really wasn't so sure of anything except that the hijackers were across the street from us, and HD and the others were gone. "I wish we had some light, Ms. Sarah, so we can see better."

"And I wish we could find a phone jack, Billy, to plug the phone in that's sitting on the office desk."

"Want me to go look for one?" Billy asked, happy to be distracted.

"Sure, leave the phone on the desk, just look around the walls for a phone jack, you know what that looks like right?"

"Like an electric socket except different, its only got one hole in the wall instead of two or three," Billy said, proud of himself for being so knowledgeable.

"Right, Mr. Smarty Pants! Now, take the flashlight, keep it down away from the window ok? Stay quiet, I think the bad people are still across the street."

"They're putting stuff in the car," Billy said, a little fear in his voice. He peeked out the window and asked, "Is the Sheriff going to get them?"

"Yes. The Sheriff is going to get them and put them in jail, I promise."

I raised myself from the floor just enough to peek out the window. Two men were coming down from the upper room of the Visitor

Center. They carried what looked to be a body down the steps. They put it in a sitting position in the jeep's driver's seat. Then they went back upstairs. This time they each carried two bags down the steps. "What's this," I whispered to myself. I watched them go back upstairs and realized that they were packing up, getting ready to leave. "Dear God," I say aloud, "they might run into the boys on the road. I must find a phone jack. Billy, come here."

"Ms. Sarah, I plugged the phone in the wall but there's no dial tone."

"Okay, did you see a big metal box on the wall in the office?"

"Yes, it's behind the desk."

"Open the box, there's switches in it," I instructed, "turn one of them on, we must get a dial tone for the phone, we must try and get a call out to the police. Those guys might run into HD and the trail runners on the road."

Billy went into the office and groped around the boxes of tourist merchandise until he got to the electric fuse box.

"Here it is!" Billy exclaimed. He flipped the biggest switch in the metal fuse box. The

Marina lit up like a Christmas tree, inside and out, and the loudspeakers above the Canteen blared out a country and western tune by Johnny Cash. "TURN IT OFF! TURN IT OFF!" I shouted, but it was too late. Billy turned the switch off and the Marina went dark and silent.

"I turned on the wrong switch! Will they come over here and try to kill us?" Billy said tearful, his voice trembled with fear.

"If they do come over here, you go in the office and get under the desk, Billy. Don't come out until I call you. Stay there, no matter what you hear, will you do that?" I tried to swallow the blood pooling in my mouth, I needed to stop moving around, "Nobody's going to kill me or you, not with this rifle here to defend us."

***

The two men stopped loading their vehicles and looked towards the Marina, one ran up the steps to the Visitor Center's upper room, and the room's dim light suddenly winked out. The other man stayed downstairs. He was interested in who was in the Marina and had set a deadly

151

glare on the vacant dark window that faced the Visitor Center.

***

"Get under the desk, Billy."

Billy scurried into the office and crawled under the desk. I sat with my back against the wall. I had a good view of the front door and the long windows that faced the pier. I hoped they would leave.

But if they didn't, I'd see them before they saw me. In a desperate effort to focus, I closed my eyes and took an excruciating deep breath that proved to be near fatal. My body was wracked with pain. I knew the less I moved the more strength I'd have in case there was a shoot-out.

There were several empty boxes next to me. I pulled them over to me, turned one upside down and rested the loaded rifle on it. I maneuvered myself such that the rifle butt was against my left shoulder. The rifle had five rounds, which included what HD loaded before he left. I have a chance. There's only two men. Dizziness

152

encompassed me, my body was feverish and ached. The probability of passing out was strong. I'm as ready as I'll ever be, "Stay alert, stay alive," I whispered to myself.

CHAPTER 21

The day before the bus hijacking, Chief Deputy Slater had gotten up early refreshed from a good night's sleep. He prepared for the morning meeting and hoped something came of yesterday's interrogations at the Tamiami Gas and Shop. He also wondered if FBI agent Russell found anything. Slater knew the Sheriff expected an update today. Slater walked into the meeting room and said, "Okay what've we got?"

Deputy Hillert gave a current run down on the missing bus, bus driver and children. He also reported on the interview with the employee at the Tamiami Gas and Shop. Hillert had written down that the green jeep Cherokee, was owned by Kyle Moleto. Its license plate number was KUL-GUY6, and the owner lived at 2141 Palm Circle, Coral Gables, Florida.

Hillert also wrote the bus number, 51, on the whiteboard behind him even though everyone already knew which bus was missing. The school had reported it yesterday afternoon when it didn't show up at the bus barn. Hillert wrote it on the board anyway. He ended his report with,

"I'll be going back today to scour the side of the road where the jeep and bus were last seen."

"Why didn't you do that yesterday, it rained last night!" Slater said, as he scowled at Hillert. "Next!" Slater said as he glared at his deputy. While Slater was embarrassing Deputy Chuck Hillert for not following up on the area across the street from the Tamiami Gas and Shop, Agent Russell looked at his list of license plates that he'd pulled out of the bank's computer data base the day before.

"What's this!"

Before Slater could introduce Deputy Pepper, Agent Russell exclaimed, "We have a match. The jeep's license plate is on this list of bank employees, KUL-GUY6, green Jeep Cherokee. It is registered to Kyle Moleto, at 2141 Palm Circle, Coral Gables, FL.

The meeting was interrupted by a knock at the door. The station secretary came into the conference room and handed a manila envelope to Slater, "Someone left this for you, Sir. I was on break when it came in and whoever left it on my desk left no name." Slater tore open the envelope and sorted through several pictures of tire tracks, a shell casing, blood-stained dirt, and footprints. He immediately realized that the pictures were apparently taken prior to the storm. A note was attached,

"I took these pictures yesterday when I left your meeting, the shell casing is still there, a short distance on Flamingo Road, everything else probably got washed away in the rain, at dawn." Signed, T.S. Macon.

Slater handed the envelope to Deputy Hillert, and between gritted teeth said, "Get down to Flamingo Road and see if there is a shell casing along the side of the road. This should have been done last night!"

Slater immediately got on the phone to Sheriff John Hampstead whose central office for Monroe County was in Key West. He filled the Sheriff in on the latest findings, the name and address of a possible suspect who happened to be an employee at the bank at the time of the Florida City bank heist. In addition, this individual was wanted for questioning regarding the disappearance of school bus 51 and the four people on the bus. It turned out that the suspect's vehicle was last seen parked on Route

41, in front of Bus 51, across from Tamiami Gas and Shop. Sheriff Hampstead notified the Metro Dade County Police and ordered a search of the Coral Gables address and a person of interest, Kyle Moleto, possibly armed and dangerous.

Kyle was long gone when the police arrived at his parents' elegant home. A typical kidnapper's profile didn't usually include wealth and prosperity. When no one answered the door, the police did not hesitate to break through heavy mahogany double doors with a battering ram. They entered the house with a warrant to search the premises.

A set of crumpled up blueprints were found in the trash can of one of the bedrooms. Sheriff Hampstead found a stash of weapons under a bed. He wondered if they were licensed to Kyle Moleto. In the garage, they discovered several pickaxes, shovels and other tools that could very well have been used to dig through the walls of the bank. Hampstead ordered a car and two officers to remain across the street in case Kyle showed up.

Later that night, in the early morning hours Chief Deputy Slater sent a chopper over the glades. He hoped that they would locate the kids and bus driver. The helicopter's huge light beams scanned the trails that could be seen from the air south from Big Banyan towards Flamingo. He had plenty of information; the whereabouts of the bus in Bear Lake, pictures taken by Mr. Macon of the gun shell casing, tire marks and bloody sand from the side of the road.

Most importantly he had the license plate number of Kyle Moleto's jeep that he got from the eyewitness at the Tamiami Gas and Shop. Slater was determined to find Moleto, and he worried about the kids and bus driver. Someone was wounded, time was running out.

CHAPTER 22

Ben meandered over to the now dark and silent Marina by way of a wooden jetty that connected it to the pier. Even in the summer months a boat or two was often moored there but tonight the pier was vacant and silent. Ben stepped onto the walkway and slowly approached the Marina.

"Whoa! Creaky wooden planks for a walkway. I bet this oughta scare Ms. Bus Driver," Ben chuckled. The rhythmic slap of water against the pilings underneath the walkway and the occasional splash of water by fish feeding close to the surface greeted him.

Ben wiped his sweaty hands on his pant leg and pulled out Kyle's gun, unaware of how few or many bullets were left in the chamber. He tucked the pistol back into the front of his jeans and said to himself, "Hmmm, this ole pistol sends a thrill down my spine, such power you give me Mr. Gun."

It was too late to wonder whether Ms. Bus Driver was hiding in the Marina or not. In fact, Ben was so sure that she was there and in a weakened and wounded state, that it didn't dawn on him to be cautious or afraid. "If you hadn't pulled up at the traffic light in the first place, you wouldn't have been shot, been no need for us to get rid of the bus, and Ms. Bus Driver, we wouldn't be down here at this god forsaken hideout. Instead, one of us should have caught a ride to town, see, bought a tire, come back and then we would have fixed the tire. We'd have gone home as was *originally* planned. We would've split the money as *originally* planned and be long gone from Florida. But nooooo, you had to mess—it–all–up. I'm angry ma'am, I'm angry and frustrated and pumped to kill you for all the trouble you caused me and my buddies."

The walkway creaked on each step. The railing was loose and wobbly in some places. Ben shined his flashlight down into the water below the walkway. In the moon light, he saw a gator snout above the water looking up at him, and the fin of a bull shark cruised amidst the schools of fish that came to feed on the night bugs and mosquitoes drawn to the water.

The air had a rotten fishy smell to it, the kind of smell when the water was at low tide. This time of night the water was only three to four

160

feet deep. "I just want out of this place—damn," Ben said as he jiggled the doorknob to the Marina. "Now I'm gonna break the glass, so I can unlock the door from the inside, you hear me Ms. Bus Driver? I'm coming for you."

Glass tinkled to the floor. Ben reached through the glass panel and turned the lock from the inside. "Why do I feel like hummin' a tune," Ben said and laughed aloud.

"I feel playful, like playing hide and seek. *Oooh, yoooo hooo*," Ben crooned softly, "are you here, Ms. Bus Driver?"

Ben hummed as he walked past the counter, and cash register. The wide faced flashlight was more than adequate for Ben to find Sarah. He walked slowly down the first row and passed the empty unplugged refrigerator unit.

His movements were slow and deliberate, and he hummed all the while. He saw nothing down the refrigerator aisle, so he aimed the flashlight against the back wall—nothing.

"I'm coming for you, Ms. Bus Driver, and I'm gonna find you ma'am. I'm heading back to the front of the store and then I'm gonna start down the second row. Come out now Ms. Bus

Driver, I promise—I'll go easy on you. You know, I'll make it quick, you won't feel a thing," he whispered.

To the tune of *Oh where oh where has my little dog gone*...Ben started down the second aisle, and passed fishhooks, fishing line, boxes of lures, some with feathers, others bright iridescent and rubbery. He passed a rack of wide brimmed hats and ball caps with long bills and a shelf of long narrow boxes with pictures of a fishing rod on the front of them. He continued to move towards the back of the store and passed more fishing tackle and an assortment of tackle boxes.

Ben made his way to the middle of the row and focused the flashlight down the rest of the aisle to the back wall—nothing... He returned to the front of the store and worked his way down the third row of merchandise. As he neared the end of the row, he came across bloody bandages and paper wrappings, strewn over the floor.

"Aha," he said as he discovered the office door, "oh, I bet you're hiding in that room, and I see you were busy with some bandages too."

He went back to the front of the last row and lit up the aisle all the way to the back wall and window. Against the wall were several boxes stacked on top of each other. Ben walked towards the office. The door was open.

"Are you in here Ms. Bus Driver?" he asked in a sing song voice. A whimper and a sniffle greeted him as he stood at the entrance to the office, "Aha! so you *are* in here!" Ben laughed.

"No, you jack ass, I'm right behind you, if you're smart, you'll get out of here fast, don't turn around just leave!"

****

Sarah's voice was full of fear. Her hands trembled and she struggled to hold the rifle Denis had given her. She had propped the rifle up on one of the boxes. Her finger was ready to squeeze the rifle's trigger.

Ben knew Sarah was right behind him, he swung around and shot in the direction of her voice, click, click no bullets. He fired again, click. "Three's a charm," Sarah said and fired back before he could shoot again. The rifle shot blew Ben off his feet, a direct hit to his chest. He fell to the floor and crawled up the aisle. At the sound of the rifle shot, Eddie hollered, "Ben! Ben!"

Ben stumbled out the Marina door staggered onto the walkway. His knees buckled, and he fell. He pulled himself up against the rail and as he staggered down the walkway, he bumped against the rail, and it gave way. Ben plunged into the water below. Disoriented he thrashed about in the inky black waters all around him, "Ben! Ben!" Eddie hollered again, "hold on!"

****

Eddie turned his truck around until the headlights lit up the churning water. Ben went under, a sharp pain sliced through his chest, and he blacked out. Eddie ran into the water and grabbed Ben by the arm and dragged him to his car. "I can't wait here for you Ben, you know they are coming for us, I have to go," Eddie said as he lifted Ben into the front seat of his car, "at least the gators won't get you if you're in the car."

Eddie felt for Ben's pulse, "you're still alive buddy. I hope you wake up before the cops find you," a twinge of guilt flashed through Eddie, "at this point pal, I hope you make it, just don't rat me out."

Eddie slammed Ben's car door shut, then jumped in his truck and sped away toward Tamiami Trail, thirty plus miles up the road. Flamingo quickly disappeared in the darkness. Eddie couldn't believe how bad the night had turned out. He had left his buddies behind, one dead the other passed out and seriously wounded. Then there's that wounded woman, with a gun, no less still alive after hours in the Everglades. "Oh God, what have I done," Eddie shouted over the roar of his truck, "Dad, you know it wasn't me, I just wanted the money for a new start." Eddie said out aloud to his long-deceased dad. "I didn't want any of this, it wasn't my idea to shoot anyone, all for what—this damn money, that's what."

Ten miles down the road, Eddie stopped the truck, got out and threw his share of the heist out on the asphalt–all 3 canvas bags. Then he thought better of it. He put the bags back in the

165

truck and drove back to Flamingo. He threw the bags out on the sandy parking lot next to the green jeep. When Eddie got back to the Visitor Center, he couldn't resist checking on Kyle, to see if his buddy was dead. He'd never seen a dead body before tonight. He looked in Kyle's jeep window and stepped back aghast. Kyle's face was grey, his head leaned against the driver's window, his dead eyes stared straight at Eddie.

Eddie wasted no time getting back in his truck. He sped away for the second time. "That's it, I'm done Dad," Eddie said, shaken by Kyle's dead stare. After a few moments, he settled down, a peaceful calm came over him.

"I did the right thing, it's all going to be okay now," he told himself as he sped down Flamingo Road. "Now if I can just get out of here." He hoped the cops would discover Kyle and Eddie and the money. He hoped they wouldn't come looking for him.

CHAPTER 23

HD, Jack and the trail runners moved quickly down Flamingo Road in a tight group. They were ever vigilant of the dangerous predators that teemed in the glades all around them. They were drenched in sweat from the dense heat and humidity. Then a sudden downpour typical of the summer in the glades gave relief from the heat yet washed away what was left of the bug repellant. The mosquitoes and night flyers left welts on the exposed areas of their bodies. HD knew it was too dark to look for the purple beauty berry leaves, a natural bug repellant that would have given them some relief from the incessant swarm of biting insects.

Jack lacked the stamina of HD and his friends. Try as he may, he just couldn't keep up with the trail runners. Several times everyone stopped and waited for Jack to catch up with them. At one point while they waited for Jack to catch up, Mark had noticed bright iridescent eyes in the pitch-black glades. Each time they slowed for Jack to catch up, the iridescent eyes appeared a few feet closer. So far, the bright glare of the flashlights and trail runners loud angry voices chased whatever it was back into the recesses of the dark glades. "We can't waste any more ammo shooting into the dark, we need to be sure we have enough in case those men come up behind us," Denis said, troubled that the glow-in-the-dark eyes continued to follow them.

A stalking predator was something Denis and Mark, two very seasoned hunters, had never experienced or seen before tonight. Generally, panthers were secretive and hard to find. But summer is the Florida Panther mating season and panthers became more aggressive and had been known to approach and challenge humans that got in their way. To make matters worse, the panthers were drawn to their mates near Flamingo Road. Denis wondered if the stalking panther saw them as a threat—that infringed on its territory or rather looked to them as prey.

"Okay, guys, pick up the pace a bit, and see if we can lose the panther," Denis ordered.

"Not to worry," Mark said, "those anacondas—are night predators too, and we should keep a look out for them as well." Mark immediately regretted blurting out something that would make everyone including himself panic. "Uh—Denis is right, let's pick up the pace a bit," Mark said. "What a stupid thing to say," Mark mumbled to himself.

Everyone followed suit, but once they stepped up the pace, they were no longer a tight group as Jack fell behind again even though he was desperate to keep up. Jack would have surely fallen to the ground exhausted were it not for the glowing eyes in the dark.

Then out of nowhere, the screech of a vehicle's brakes on pavement and a loud blare of a horn came up behind them. "Get in," Eddie shouted as he pulled up next to Jack.

Everyone ran towards the vehicle and jumped into the truck bed relieved to be off the road. No one recognized Eddie's truck as the truck that was parked at the Visitors Center across from the Marina. It never dawned on them that the truck's driver was one of the men who hijacked the bus, rather everyone thought he was part of a rescue team.

****

Jack jumped in the front seat. Without another word Eddie sped down the road. He thought the men he picked up were night hunters and Eddie was glad to do something good for a change. It felt good to help. He looked over at Jack and asked, "What's your name?"

"Jack, Jack Weller."

"Hang tight," Eddie said, "I'll get you and your buddies to the main road. I thought night hunters didn't hunt during the summer months."

"Someone stole my bus and tried to kill the bus driver!" Jack exclaimed. "If it hadn't been for HD we would've been killed by those rotten guys. They not only stole the bus they dumped it in Bear Lake too!"

Eddie drove in silence, and thought to himself, "So, there *were* people besides the bus driver on the bus the other day. She lied about that."

Eddie clearly recalled Kyle asking Sarah who else was on the bus, "No one," she had said. "Why didn't we see them?" Eddie wondered.

Eddie felt a sudden sense of dread. The idea of an escape was suddenly remote. "If only Ben had stayed away from the Marina, but then again, these guys would have been on the road anyway, and idiot Ben would have probably killed them in cold blood, just for the hell of it," Eddie cringed at the thought of it all.

"Thanks for rescuing us," Jack said, "you came in the nick of time, I was losing ground, couldn't keep up, so tired."

"Did anyone find the bus?" Eddie asked.

"The trail runners found it and called it in yesterday."

Eddie looked through the rearview mirror, "Are they the trail runners in the back, were any of them on the bus with you when it got hijacked?" Eddie asked.

"Uh, only HD was on the bus with me. Billy is down at the Marina with Miss Sarah, the bus driver. She's sick, she got shot you see. HD says they'll send a helicopter out. Probably head down Flamingo Road to the Marina, then come after us. But you've found us already, aren't you going to call it in?" Jack asked.

"Oh, well I would, but my cell phone died a while back, so I can call it in when we get to Route 41, at the Tamiami Gas and Shop, you know the one across the road? So uh, the bus driver and how many people were on the bus?"

"Me and two other boys," Jack said. "HD is the oldest, and he saved our lives, he saw the hijackers. HD had us hide in the back of the bus near the EXIT door, that's how we escaped."

"Where did you escape?"

"We rolled out the back of the bus on Bear Lake Trail, right before they sunk the bus in the lake."

Feigning ignorance Eddie asked, "So, why did they take the bus?"

"I don't know, we were on the way home from school see, and Miss Sarah, the bus driver, was at a stop light and the next thing I know is HD is pulling us to the back of the bus, me and Billy, so we hunched down under the back seats and the next thing we hear is—bang! Someone shot Sarah, then after a few minutes they threw her down the aisle of the bus. I thought she was dead, but she wasn't, thank God for that. I heard a lot of mean yelling—it was awful."

As Jack laid bare everything that Kyle and Ben did, all Eddie could think about was how he was going to escape now. Eddie noticed that when he picked up the other guys that some of them had rifles. He wondered if they've figured out who he is yet. He wondered if they recognized his truck as being parked outside the Visitor Center across from the Marina. "Uh, Jack, listen did you see anything else before you left Flamingo?" Eddie asked in a calm voice tone. "Well," Jack started, "when we got to Flamingo it was night, and pitch-black, except for the light from a window at the Visitor Center. There were a couple cars parked in front of it."

"How many cars did you see?"

"I think there was three, no two cars and a truck, yea that's it, but we didn't hang around for long, because we could hear them shouting and arguing. So, we went out the back door of the Marina and escaped into the dark, they never knew we were there."

"What color did you say the truck was?"

"I didn't see, I didn't notice what color anything was, it was too dark. Why are you asking about the color of the truck, what diff—"

****

Jack stopped talking mid-sentence. He had a
sudden feeling that he said too much. He
repeated over and over to himself what he said
to Eddie—two cars and a truck, two cars and a
truck.

Silence filled the truck cab like thick mud.
Jack realized that he's not out of this nightmare
yet. In fact, it felt like things are going to get
worse. He sensed that the guy sitting next to him
could be one of the guys that hurt Sarah, stole
the bus, and dumped it. "Not again," Jack said
to himself as the truck sped down Flamingo
Road towards Tamiami Trail.

***

Grateful for the dark, Eddie realized no one
recognized him or his truck, not until now,
"Should have kept my mouth shut," Eddie
thought to himself, "and not asked that question
about the color of the truck at the Marina. Now,
I need to do something with this kid and the
guys in the back. I'm no killer and since I have
no money bags—but Jack did figure out who I
am," Eddie thought to himself, and he wished he

could kill them. But then Eddie realized they have rifles. Sadly, he knew that if he posed a threat to them, they might shoot him. He hoped to get them to Tamiami Gas and Shop and then disappear into the night. He hoped no one would ask why he was in the glades, in the middle of the night, on Flamingo Road.

CHAPTER 24

Hidden by darkness, tears of exhaustion and fear ran down Jack's cheeks. He looked straight ahead and dared not turn his head to look at the man driving.

"How much further is it to Tamiami Gas and Shop?" Jack asked fearfully.

"Oh, I figure about ten minutes away," Eddie said, no emotion in his voice.

"That's where you're taking us, right?" said Jack, but Eddie did not respond.

Now racked with terror Jack looked out his window, the truck was moving at about 50 miles per hour. He wondered if it would kill him if he rolled out of the truck, the way he rolled out of the bus. He checked to see if his door was locked, then groped around the door panel for the handle, it was easy to find. His movements were calculated and slow, so as not to distract Eddie. Jack waited a few more minutes, gathered his courage, "Roll when you hit the ground," Jack said to himself, "like HD told us back at the lake before they rolled out of the bus on Bear Lake Trail." But the bus was only moving about 10-15 miles per hour. "God—

don't let me die," Jack prayed as he threw open the truck door and prepared to jump. Eddie slammed on the brakes, Jack rolled out of the moving truck, hit the black asphalt road, and rolled as far from the truck as he could.

"Get out, get out!" Jack screamed, "He's one of the robbers!" The men in the back of the truck were thrown forward and banged against the truck cab window. Eddie swerved to control the truck and slammed on the brakes. It was not enough to stop the truck before it crashed into a tree across the road. His body propelled forward, through the windshield and his head hit hard against a tree. Unconscious, the rest of Eddie's body lay across the hood of the truck his body crinkled, like an accordion. Tendrils of smoke rose from the engine—whump, a small fire ignited under the hood.

Everyone staggered out of the bed of the truck, except Denis who was knocked out. Mark, Joel, and Chris pulled him from the truck and dragged him to safety. HD ran to the front of the truck, yanked Eddie off the burning hood and pulled him toward the others. They all lay in a heap, on the asphalt road, as a ball of flame engulfed the truck.

Their faces glistened with blood and sweat in the light of the flames, HD sat on the asphalt shaking his head and talking to himself.

***

"Jack can't be right," HD said to no one, "why would anyone be driving on Flamingo Road in the middle of a pitch-black night?" HD's mind wandered, still in shock, "some people do fish at night, but not so much in the summer months, not here in the glades. I can't believe that truck was the one parked back at the Visitor Center with the other two cars. I was glad he picked us up, hoped he'd drop us off at the highway, but maybe not—I figured we'd be safe either way, he knew we had rifles," HD reasoned.

HD got up and staggered over to Jack, who was sprawled out on the asphalt. He moaned as he held his broken arm. "It's him, it's him, HD, I'm sure of it, I woulda' never jumped out of the truck if it had been otherwise. He kept asking about the cars at the Visitor Center and after I said it was two cars and a truck, he asked did I see what color the truck was, and I... I... panicked and this horrible feeling came over me like he was gonna kill us, I just panicked," Jack sobbed as he held his broken arm.

"Jack! Get a hold of yourself—lots of people come out here and fish in the lakes and lagoons. Flamingo Road has at least six or seven side roads. You just panicked—and believe me I've had enough of this nightmare too."

HD put his hand on Jack's chest to calm him, the way his father would put his hand on his chest when he was afraid or in a fight with school bullies and had come home beat up and freaked out.

Thirteen-year- old Jack put his hands over HD's and said, "Thank God for you HD, wish you were my brother or friend." Jack turned his head and wept silently. HD leaned over, "See if you can get on my back."

Jack sat up. He held his broken arm close to his body. He put his good arm around HD's neck and HD pulled Jack to his feet and hoisted him piggyback style onto his back.

Denis came to, a little dizzy but okay. He and Mark leaned over Eddie sprawled out on the road, alive but unconscious. "He's alive. We need to get him to Tamiami as quick as we can," Mark said, "We can take turns carrying him, I'll go first."

Mark hoisted Eddie over his shoulder and all together Joel and Chris quickly walked around the burning truck. Once the truck was behind them, they started to walk/jog again. This time intent on a non-stop hike to Tamiami Trail. As they gained distance from the fire, the light waned; and darkness enveloped them once again, Joel and Chris lit the way with flickering flashlights, a sure sign the batteries are getting low.

A sudden swoosh of air blew past them. Tree branches swayed, their leaves a sudden chaos of movement and whispers. The wind was a welcome reprieve from the stifling humidity of the hot summer night. A bluish white lightning bolt hit right smack in the middle of the road, not fifteen feet from the straggling group of men with a deafening crack of thunder that resounded through the glades. The smell of ozone and rain filled the air. Within seconds, the men were pelted by heavy sheets of rain and there was no shelter from the summer storm. With their heads down, the trail runners kept stride through the rain and maintained an uncanny stamina unique to them, unique to the Seminole men. The sudden summer storm lasted half an hour before it started to subside.

Rivulets of rushing rainwater were everywhere on either side of the road draining into the glades. Tree branches hung low, and the sound of dripping water was all around. Once the rains subsided, mist rose out of the trees and steam swirled around Flamingo Road. They stopped long enough for Joel to relieve Mark and take Eddie over his shoulder.

Darkness was giving way to a dim light and the road ahead slowly revealed itself. As the night sounds faded away with the morning dawn a few birds began to chirp. Gradually, the glades were filled with bird calls and their chaotic chatter. From behind the weary haggard group of men, somewhere in the distance, the whump whump of helicopter propellers could be heard.

CHAPTER 25

Six hours earlier, Big Banyan's Chief of Police, Paul Bowman, waited anxiously to hear from the trail runners. "It's midnight, can't wait any longer boys," Bowman announced to his officers, (referring to the trail runners who went after the kidnapped children and bus driver.) Bowman looked at the wall map in the main conference room.

He traced his finger from Bear Lake over Bear Lake Trail to Bear Lake Road, he then traced it to Flamingo Road. Like Denis, he too wondered why HD took to the glades, "They'd have to hike around the mangroves which would have led them to the nearest hammock, and through dry, waist high grasslands," Chief Bowman said to himself.

Bowman knew the trail was hard to find and God help them if they ran into one of the snakes, big cats, or wild hogs. "The panthers won't go after them at least until dark. There's been no attacks reported in a couple years. Well, other than the time a toddler wandered off—not sure whether it was a panther or bobcat that got him."

Bowman continued to trace the trail through the hammock south to the now deserted campgrounds of Flamingo. Talking to himself, Bowman said, "If they stay on the hammock trail, it should take them directly to the Flamingo ghost town. There, the children would have had access to fresh water. Damn long hike," Bowman sighed "I sure hope they've all survived. Slater will want to get divers to Bear Lake and check out the bus. No calls from the boys yet— cell phones probably out of range."

Bowman rubbed his chin in a worrisome kind of way. He called Slater and reported the trail runner's findings at Bear Lake. "When the bus was reported missing, I sent trackers out to find them. They found the school bus submerged in Bear Lake. There is evidence of survivors; remains of three campfires, some fish heads and two handmade fishing poles. They also reported that HD Macon left signs that he entered the glades. I've recently lost contact with my trackers, but I suspect HD has gone around the lake and south towards Flamingo ghost town. That's a days' hike and fresh water is there."

"Uh huh," Slater said, "I'll send forensics down to Bear Lake."

****

Slater hung up and sat on the edge of his bed. He dialed headquarters, "We need a forensics crew at Bear Lake and a helicopter rescue. The rescue team is to fly south to the Flamingo ghost town then follow Flamingo Road north to include the Visitor Center and Marina."

Slater summed up the current information which included the missing school bus now submerged in the lake and that there may be bodies in the bus. According to Bowman's trackers, there is evidence that Tommie Macon's boy took to the glades and around the lake, south to Flamingo ghost town.

Slater headed to the office and briefed his deputies. One of the deputies asked, "So, who are we looking for?"

"We're looking for a female bus driver and three kids ages 18, 13, and 8. The bus has been located, we need to get the bus out of Bear Lake and check for bodies. One other thing, we have

184

reason to believe the person involved in the bank robbery hijacked the bus and kidnapped the kids and bus driver. An employee of the bank has license plates that match the plates of a jeep that was seen in front of the bus before it disappeared. We have an APB out on the car now and the house has been searched. No money has turned up yet, however plenty of evidence has been confiscated and sent to forensics for finger printing and DNA." Slater paused a moment then continued instructions to his deputies, "There's a chance you may run into the perp. Aside from having the bank money, he may be armed and dangerous."

At 2 o'clock in the morning, the bus was pulled from the brackish waters of Bear Lake. At first light divers searched the lake for bodies.

"No bodies in the bus, sir, I found two back packs and a lunchbox and around the driver's seat we found a purse."

"Nothing else?" Slater asked.

"No sir, that's it."

"Get everything to the Lab," Slater ordered as he put his hand to his portable 2-way radio transceiver, "Call in a rescue helicopter to land at Big Banyan Police Department. I'll meet you there."

When Slater and three of his deputies arrived at the Station, Police Chief Bowman was there waiting for them. Slater was aghast at the thought of anyone stranded in the glades, "My God, I can't imagine hiking through the glades in the dead of night, let alone the summer rainy season."

Slater, his three deputies, Bowman and Ronnie Tigertail quickly boarded the helicopter. "The best way to Flamingo from here is south through the hammocks," Bowman explained, "the park trail is visible from the air. Even so, it's carved straight down the middle of the southern-most hammock, that's where we're headed, and that's the path we hope the trail runners took to Flamingo."

Bowman didn't think anyone needed to know about the hidden trail that Big Banyan hunters use and have used for several hundred years.

"Who are the trail runners?" Slater asked.

"A couple of men I called to track perps who think they can hide in the glades. My men know the expanse of the Everglades better than anyone, except maybe my sons, Joel, and Chris, who are out there too," Bowman said. Slater nodded at Bowman, "I am grateful for that."

"They grew up in the glades. If the bus driver and kids are out there, I'm confident they'll find them, I am quite proud of my sons."

As the helicopter rose, huge flood lights beamed down over the river of grass and illuminated a path south towards the Wilderness Water Way. An hour into the flight, they passed over the Waterway, found the park trail, and followed it over the hammock that stretched south to Florida Bay.

They flew low and the high grass leaned away, against the force of the helicopter's blades. The trail was in plain view from the air. Night predators ran away from the loud flying machine that bore down on them. An anaconda, two feet wide and twenty-five feet long slithered through the grasses, away from the powerful headlights that exposed its nocturnal hunt.

CHAPTER 26

Meanwhile, back at the Marina, Ben woke to a sharp stabbing pain in his chest. In addition, the windows to his late model Toyota sedan were closed and the heat was stifling, his body was drenched in sweat and throbbed with pain. As he continued to gain consciousness, he began to remember things. He recalled the blast that hit him and falling into the Bay.

"How'd I get in my car?" Ben looked out the rearview mirror at the Marina, all was dark and quiet. Ben glanced over at the jeep and where the truck had been parked. "Eddie's truck is gone," he said aloud, "Kyle looks like he's asleep. Man—what's, up with that?"

Ben groaned as he remembered the shoot-out with Kyle, how he and Eddie put Kyle's dead body upright in his jeep, "Yea Kyle that's what you get for being you," Ben moaned, "ugh, someone shot me, better get out of here, uh what's with this pain?" Ben touched the wound in his chest. "Gotta get outta here," he whined.

"Where's my money," he said to no one, and looked in the back seat, then wondered if he put it in the trunk, "I'll have to get out to check.

Damn I'm dizzy, okay—one thing at a time—ugh! I can't move. Okay then I'll fall out."

Ben slowly opened the car door and quietly fell forward onto the ground. He crawled to the back of his car. He noticed that there were several canvas bags strewn on the ground. He grabbed two of the bags, dragged them to the side of his car, opened the door and threw them into the backseat. Searing pain cut through his chest, nausea overwhelmed him, and he doubled over. "I can hardly breathe, geez it hurts."

Ben pulled himself into the driver's seat. He sucked in air and coughed up blood that trickled from the side of his mouth. He started the car and without the aid of headlights he quietly backed out of the parking lot. Then, he slowly drove away from the Marina and into the pitch black of night with only the crunch of gravel and the smoothness of the asphalt road to guide him.

Ben was terrified that he'd get shot in the back of his head as he drove passed the Marina. "I'm hurtin' and this headache—must have hit my head and then—what, fell in the water? Shoot, I'm lucky a gator didn't get me, don't remember anything else, I wonder who put me in the car, did I get in myself?"

Ben drove intent on getting out of the glades. Behind him the *whump whump* of helicopter propeller blades came closer and closer. Fortunately, his car was no longer in the range of its search lights. He continued down Flamingo Road without headlights, slow and easy. Every now and then he felt the car go over the road onto the soft shoulder.

When he could no longer hear the helicopter, (perhaps it landed at the Marina,) Ben opened the car door and with the aid of the car's interior lights Ben hung out to see the repeating white lines painted on the asphalt to keep him on the road. He managed to creep along until he came to a sign on the right side of the road. He grabbed his flashlight and shined it on a street sign that read, *Flamingo Cove 5 miles ahead.* An arrow pointed to the right.

Flamingo Cove was one of many pools, lakes, ponds, and lagoons fed by the plentiful rain and saltwater of the Florida Bay, which was only a short walk from the Cove. Ben turned onto the side road and turned on the headlights.

Ben drove the five miles to the end of the road which opened to a spacious sandy beach around a pool of water surrounded by tropical foliage.

With just his headlights, Ben saw the moon's reflection on the surface of the pool and it was beautiful. "I'll hide and rest here until all the commotion calms down, my head—so much pain," he moaned.

Ben laid his head back on the head rest and fell asleep only to be jolted awake at the crack and boom of thunder around him, followed by a heavy downpour. "Damn lucky I'm in the car, safe here—the car tires will ground me." The summer storm was a bit like a freak show.

Every few seconds, lightning lit up the area and revealed the Cove in greater detail. The rainwater flowed from all around into the pool until it overflowed and flooded the surrounding area. Within minutes, the pool had swelled to twice its original size. If it swelled any more, Ben's tires would be underwater, he knew he'd have to back up. When the rains stopped, the edge of the pool had swollen to a foot from Ben's front fender.

Ben rolled down the window. A gentle wind, cool and fresh rushed across his face. The fragrance from something blooming close by lingered in the air. He sighed and suddenly felt relaxed. He was certain he was safe here and decided to stay a while. "In the morning, I'll move on, skip town, head for the Bahamas and beyond. I'm on my way to a life of wealth. I can afford anything now, the nicest house, cars, maybe a Harley motorcycle—anything, just like that fool Kyle. Yea," Ben whispered, "I'm as good as Kyle, rich and poor no more."

As the clouds moved towards Florida Bay, a clear starry sky sparkled in the darkness. Ben looked up at the tiny lights, "Poor no more," he repeated. His gaze fixed on the celestial pool of stars. Ben took a painful breath and exhaled for the last time.

CHAPTER 27

"Ms. Sarah, Ms. Sarah, I think they're all gone. It's real quiet over there," Billy whispered. He patted Sarah's good arm. "Please don't be dead Ms. Sarah. Wake up," he cried. In the distance Billy heard an incoming helicopter.

"I think there's a helicopter outside; can you hear it?" Billy said.

After shooting Ben, Sarah had collapsed, and this time Billy could tell she wasn't going to wake up anytime soon. Billy cried. He was afraid that Sarah was dead. As the helicopter drew closer and closer, Billy ran to the office and turned on the main switch. The Marina lit up and country music blared out over the pier, an odd welcome to their rescuers. The helicopter beams lit up the Visitor Center and Marina.

***

Slater looked down. A jeep was parked in front of the Visitor Center and several canvas bags lay in heap around the vehicle. As the helicopter began its descent, a small boy could be seen running up and down the rickety Marina pier walkway, waving frantically and crying. The helicopter landed easily and without incident on the hard-packed sand in front of the Marina. Slater made note of the jeep and its tags. They matched the description on his report; green jeep, license tags KUL-GUY6. He also spotted the canvas bags on the ground and ordered several deputies to search the Visitor Center and the rooms upstairs.

Billy ran up to Slater and clung to Slater's leg, "I'm so glad you're here, Sarah's inside and she won't wake up."

Billy chattered hysterically. Slater knelt on the sandy ground and quietly listened to the small boy until he finally broke down and wept. Slater put his arm around Billy and comforted him as best he could. "I'm calling your mama right now Billy, and you will be home in no time. Now I want you to stay with Officer Rudy here, and let me tend to Sarah, okay?" Billy nodded and looked over at Officer Rudy who held out his hand to him, "Come on I'll show you the inside of the helicopter."

Slater and Bowman approached the Marina, guns drawn, not sure what to expect. The inside lights revealed a messed-up tackle store. Merchandise was strewn everywhere. At the back of the store, amidst large empty boxes, Sarah lay unconscious, ashen faced and feverish. When Bowman checked her pulse, it was faint. She was in desperate need of medical attention. Bowman called the Tamiami Memorial Hospital, to alert them that they will be bringing in a gunshot victim. One of the deputies was also an EMT and went to work on Sarah; he set up intravenous fluids, oxygen, secured her to a stretcher and rushed her to the helicopter.

Two deputies cautiously climbed the side stairs of the Center. The door at the head of the stairs hung wide open. They set evidence markers around spent gun shells, blood stains and other evidence left behind by the hijackers. Then they secured the site with yellow tape.

Once Slater had Sarah and Billy secured in the helicopter, he and Ronnie Tigertail approached the jeep from behind. Even amid the commotion and roar of the helicopter, the man in the jeep appeared to be asleep. Slater called out to him several times, "Get out of the jeep, hands up, and lay face down on the ground."

When there was no response, several deputies approached the jeep with caution. When they reached the driver's window, it was clear that the man in the jeep was dead and had been dead for several hours. Slater called for a forensics team to helicopter out to the Flamingo Visitor Center to retrieve the dead body.

Slater walked around the jeep several times, and, by the large lights from the helicopter and Marina, discovered the tire tracks of two other vehicles. Powerful lightning strikes heralded an impending summer storm and Slater quickly took pictures of the tire tracks, that would otherwise be washed away by the time the forensics team arrived.

Everyone took to the helicopter until the storm passed. Slater wanted to question Sarah and was anxious for her to come around. It didn't take him long to realize it wouldn't be tonight. So, he decided to see what Billy had to say. Amazed and proud of this little boy who is now preoccupied with holding Sarah's limp hand, Slater joined Billy while the storm came through the area. "Billy can you tell me anything about the person who is parked next to the Visitor Center?"

"Well," Billy said timidly, "mostly there was a lot of shouting when we first got here, then it sounded like they were shooting guns. That stopped after a while, then Sarah and I saw two guys carry another guy down the stairs and put him in the jeep." Slater and Bowman looked at each other, unaware that there was more than one person at the Visitor Center. Billy continued, "Sarah wanted to look around for a phone jack and when I flipped one of the switches in the electrical box, I accidently turned the lights and music on. Sarah said turn them off, which I did. Sarah said we had to be quiet and not make any noise. She was afraid it would make the men over there angry, and it did. One of the men came over here, he sounded real mean, saying things in a hissy kind of way, and I was so scared. Sarah told me to hide under the desk, but I could still hear him talking and then he came in the office. I could hear his shoes scuffing on the floor, then Sarah shouted something and then I heard a click, click sound, then another click, then boom! Then, there was a loud noise in the front of the store and then I don't know what happened I was just too scared to even open my eyes."

Billy wiped his eyes and continued, "I remember hearing water splash and shouting voices, car doors slamming shut, then somebody drove away. After that it got quiet over there. So, I came out of my hiding place, and I saw Sarah asleep on the floor." Billy looked down at Sarah as she breathed steady through her oxygen mask, "She's still sleeping," Billy whispered.

Nothing more was said after Billy gave his account. Slater wondered who the other guys were that Billy was talking about and turned to Bowman and Ronnie Tigertail, "So according to this little boy, there is more than one kidnapper. At least three men, and Sarah shot one of them. So, where are the other two men?"

Once the storm subsided, the deputies continued to search the area for evidence and finished taping it off as a crime scene. The pilot revved up the helicopter and everyone boarded except three deputies who stayed behind to wait for the forensic team to arrive.

The night had given way to dawn when the helicopter set down on Flamingo Road. Slater and Bowman were greeted by Bowman's sons. Mark and Denis each had a man over their shoulder. HD carried a young teen, piggyback. The weary storm-soaked group turned around and faced the landing helicopter. Everyone talked at once, so relieved to be rescued.

Slater had a million questions for Denis and Mark. Chief Bowman hugged his sons and shook HD's hand. The deputy med tech assessed the condition of Jack, and the truck driver then loaded them both on board the helicopter. Then the pilot announced, "We can't carry everyone but keep walking and I'll come back for you as soon as I get these people to the hospital. We got some folks in critical condition here."

"I want to stay with HD," Jack moaned.

"No Jack, you must get that arm looked at, HD will be there shortly. Your mom's waiting for you," Slater said.

The helicopter lifted off and flew out of sight. It returned within an hour and picked up the rest of the men. Everyone was admitted through the ER and Slater made sure no one left until everyone gave a statement as to their account of the past forty-eight hours.

HD's parents met him at the ER entrance. Tommie Storm Macon held HD in his arms, and pressed his son to his chest as though he was trying to absorb HD into himself. His eyes filled with tears. So great was his relief that HD was alive. Exhausted parents greeted Jack and Billy with tears, hugs, kisses, and intense relief now that the kids and bus driver were found and, the bus recovered. However, no one was there to greet Sarah and the unconscious truck driver.

Slater was intent on finding out who and where the kidnappers were that Billy had mentioned. The truck driver, who was unknown at this time, had to be questioned. However, he was in critical condition in the ICU hospital unit.

Slater wondered who the truck driver was, there was no ID on his body or in his clothes. Everything that was in the truck was incinerated, when it blew up. Everyone who rode with the unknown man (Eddie), had to be questioned too.

Slater ordered prints on the truck driver. A comparison on the tire tread of the truck and the tire tracks at the Visitor Center, was a no go, as the tracks were washed away by the storm.

Slater realized that the unconscious man— might be a good guy—and not involved in the kidnapping or the robbery. "I must be patient and not jump to conclusions in thinking the unknown man was involved in the kidnapping."

Still, Slater wanted the truck driver to be detained until forensics examined the burned-out truck against the forensic results found in the Visitor Center. Meanwhile, Slater took stock of evidence recovered so far; a school bus retrieved from Bear Lake, a body in the morgue presumed to be Kyle Moleto, his jeep with tag KUL-GUY6.

A gun was found in Moleto's jeep. Four canvas bags with an unknown quantity of cash was found in front of the Flamingo Visitor Center. Considering the canvas bags had the bank's logo printed on them, Slater was confident that the money was from the bank robbery.

Slater also had a hunting rifle that one of his deputies recovered from the Marina. It lay across Sarah's lap. The rifle was identified and belonged to one of the trail runners. Finally, a burned-out truck whose owner may well be one of the kidnappers/robbers who was currently unconscious in ICU, his name unknown. Thoughts swirled around in Slaters' head.

He called the office, "I want Flamingo Road taped from Tamiami Trail to the Visitor Center. Absolutely no access to anyone except police personnel. Send two deputy cars to patrol the road and the side roads all the way down to the ghost campground past the Visitor Center, we're looking for anything suspicious."

CHAPTER 28

The 13-foot, 600-pound alligator whose body was submerged raised his nose above water that flooded beyond the pool. The gator's gaze was on the parked car at the edge of his deep pool. The sweet smell of death was in the air. He slowly lumbered out of the water and crawled with quiet deliberation towards the vehicle.

The dead thing was closer, but the gator couldn't see it. He pulled himself up above the hood of the car and peered into the window. Slowly, he slid back down and crawled under the car as though to claim the vehicle and the dead thing as his own. Instinctively, he waited.

***

Further down Flamingo Road, Deputies Rudy Pepper and Jimmy Danner argued as to who caught the biggest fish at the Everglades Annual Fishing Tournament last week.

"In the category of bass species, you cannot include the Peacock Bass because, it's not a bass. It's not indigenous to the Everglades," Rudy argued.

"How do you know, no one has ever told me that it is not indigenous to the glades," Jimmy argued back, "tell that to Bob Darnell and his wife, because they're pretty upset that they didn't win with the twenty pounder they pulled in."

"Well Jimmy," Rudy said, "it's the facts. The Peacock Bass is not a bass, okay? It's a South American tropical fish that thrives in the Amazon River and it's not related to any North American bass."

"You don't know that to be true," Jimmy said.

"I do know that to be true," Rudy exclaimed, "the last issue of Everglades Fisherman had a big article on the Peacock Bass and its origins. You must accept the fact that it's not a real bass like the black bass, or the largemouth bass and so on. It's an Amazonian fish, an aggressive fighter that breaks lines and screws up your tackle. That doesn't mean it's not a fun catch and good eatin', it just means it's not a real North American Bass and can't be judged as such."

The two deputies continued to argue over the Peacock Bass as they cruised down the side roads of Flamingo Road. "How many roads have we covered so far," Jimmy asked.

"Flamingo Cove Road will be the seventh. It's coming up on the right." Rudy turned onto the side road and slowly drove the short distance to the end.

"There's good fishing here in this pool, I've been down here with my boy, and we caught some nice big ones. It's one of the deepest pools on this side of the road," Rudy said.

"Whoa, hold on Rudy, looks like we have a visitor, there's not supposed to be anyone out here, not since Slater cordoned off Flamingo Road," Jimmy said as he called into headquarters to report an occupant in a car, it's license plate, and color.

Rudy stopped a good hundred feet behind the car. He sounded the siren once, but there was no movement in or around the car. The deputies wait a few more minutes. During this time, dispatch called back to them the name of the owner of the car, Ben Sykes. The deputies pulled up closer to the car and got out. Jimmy called out to the man in the car through his mega-phone but only silence answered him.

With weapons drawn, the police officers approached the vehicle. The primordial creature that had claimed the car and its dead passenger as its own, hissed a greeting to them from under the car.

"Watch out!" Rudy shouted. Jimmy shot his gun into the air. The gator, hesitant to give up his claim, charged Jimmy who backed stepped from the monster, tripped and fell backwards. The gator clenched onto Jimmy's leg and dragged him to the pool—"Get it off me, get it off me!"

Rudy fired two shots at the alligator before it unclenched its jaws and receded into the pool without its prey. "You alright?" Rudy yelled, as he sat Jimmy up. His pant leg was torn and puncture wounds from the gnarly teeth of the alligator filled with blood.

Rudy ripped the pant leg already torn and made a tourniquet for Jimmy's thigh then hoisted his partner up and walked him to the patrol car, "I'll call this in," Jimmy said, as he winced at his leg's jagged wound, "go check out the car."

Rudy walked back to the car and checked out the man who never flinched during the gator attack. Ben's dead blank eyes and ashen face stared back at Rudy. The officer found a handgun next to the corpse whose shirt was bloodied. The dead man had a gunshot wound through his chest. Rudy went around to the back seat and found two canvas bags loaded with cash. He noticed the bank logos stamped on the canvas bags. He also found a duffel bag of clothes in the trunk, "Slater said that there might be more than one perp, so far this makes two. I'll bet this guy is one of the men who robbed the bank the other day."

Jimmy called headquarters and reported their findings at Flamingo Cove. Slater was quick to respond, "I'll send a forensics team out to pick up the body and case the area for more evidence."

"Tell forensics to watch out for the gator in the pool," Rudy warned, "he's big and mean."

As soon as the forensics team arrived, the two deputies went back to town. Rudy dropped

Jimmy off at the ER and headed to the office with the canvas bags of cash.

****

Slater sized up the facts; to date they've got two corpses in the morgue who he believed were affiliated with the bank heist and the bus hijacking. He's got Ms. Sarah Miller, the bus driver, in ICU along with a 'John Doe' truck driver. "I'm not sure about the truck driver," Slater thought to himself, "even with Billy's testimony, I need more evidence to charge the John Doe with the kidnapping and heist."

Anxious to get their statements, Slater headed over to the hospital to check on HD and to see whether Ms. Sarah Miller and the truck driver were conscious. Slater had completed his questioning of the trail runners whose statements bore some similarity to what Billy had said about the goings on at the Visitor Center and Marina.

The trail runners backed up the little boy's statement. Denis and the others left prior to when Billy turned on the lights and music like

Billy said, and *before* Sarah shot a man. So, Slater figured that the only one who knew who shot the man who entered the Marina store was Sarah and no one knows who shot the guy in the jeep.

Meanwhile, the kids and the trail runners received treatment for exhaustion, dehydration, scrapes, cuts, insect bites and burns from the truck fire. Jack had to have his broken arm set in a cast and Denis, who had been thrown from the truck and knocked out, was treated for a concussion. They were all discharged except HD, who was kept behind with Billy and Jack. As for Eddie and Sarah, they are still unconscious.

CHAPTER 29

Dannie HD Macon was up and dressed for the day. He sat in a chair near the window and looked out at the Royal Palms that lined the main driveway to the hospital entrance. Slater knocked then entered HD's room. HD turned and smiled a weary smile. "Hey Danny."

"Call me HD, everyone else does."

HD extended his hand to Slater who looked up at the tall, broad shouldered eighteen-year-old Native American, "How're you feeling HD?"

"I'm tired, sore, and real hungry. Anger and fear just roils around inside me. I wonder if it will ever go away."

"I'll send out for some hamburgers and fries if you like."

"No, I'm good, just waiting for my dad to pick me up."

"Well, that should be real soon, I just need to get a statement from you. Can you give your account of what happened from the time the bus went missing, and now?"

"Dad said this was coming, that I would have to tell you about it," HD shook his head, "it was a terrible ordeal, not just for me but for Ms. Sarah who was so brave, she tried to protect us from them. She was forced to open the bus doors at gun point. She shouted back at us to hide, and the other boys didn't hear her or understand what was going on, so I ran up the aisle of the bus and grabbed them. We hid in the back of the bus before she would open the bus doors and let them in."

HD continued and recalled the entire horror of the past few days. Everything began to fall into place, and Slater jotted everything down. The high school senior paused in his recollection of the nightmare of the past 48 hours. "He doesn't know it," Slater thought to himself, "but this kid is having a delayed reaction, he's still in shock."

"The guy named Kyle convinced the others to dump the bus with Sarah's body in one of the lakes in the glades. That's when he drove out to Bear Lake. That's where we made our escape, all of us including Sarah, who they thought was dead. On Bear Lake Trail, we rolled out the back door. The trail is rarely used these days since they shut down the Flamingo campgrounds, so it's overgrown and the bus went through a lot of vines and roots that protruded from the ground. The trail is too narrow to accommodate a vehicle the size of a school bus, thank God. It provided a distraction such that they didn't even notice what we were doing. We slipped out of the slow-moving bus, dropped down onto the trail and ran into the glades far enough that we couldn't see the trail, which meant that they couldn't see us."

"So, they dumped the bus, and they walked back to the main road?"

"Yes, that's exactly what they did, we heard them talking as to what they were going to do when they passed by us."

"Did Sarah still have her gun on her?"

"I don't know what happened to her gun, she didn't have it when we escaped."

"Why didn't you take the road back to the highway, why did you go around the lake?"

"Well, I was afraid we would run into those men and that—they would kill us."

Slater stopped for a moment and tried to envision what HD had just told him. "Do you remember the names of the other two men?"

"I do. The one who laughed when Kyle shot Sarah, his name is Ben. The other guy who was constantly being shouted at by Kyle and Ben, his name is Eddie, of the three he was the only one who was against everything they did. He didn't do anything to stop the other guys though."

Slater wrote down the two names, already aware that the two bodies in the morgue were identified as Ben Sykes and Kyle Moleto. "I want you to identify them HD, do you think you can do that?"

"I didn't know they'd been captured."

"Well, we have two bodies in the morgue, one was found in a green jeep outside the Visitor Center, the other body showed up this morning in a car parked at the end of Flamingo Cove Road, at the edge of the pool.

"What about the third guy?"

"We have the man you boys pulled out of the truck, he's unconscious up in the ICU. We don't know if he was night fishing and happened upon you all or if he's the third man."

HD rubbed his hands together, a pensive expression on his face, "Jack thinks it's one of the guys, but I can't be sure until I see him. He gave us a ride and he was unarmed, but Jack jumped out of the car. It swerved into a tree and caught fire; the man was thrown through the windshield."

"Why did Jack jump out of the car?

"Something the man said spooked Jack, he kept asking questions about the cars parked in front of the Visitor Center, I don't know, you'd have to ask Jack."

"We've jumped ahead, HD, going back to your time at Bear Lake Trail, after you hid from the men, and after they were gone, what happened next?"

"It was too late in the day to go anywhere, and I was afraid we'd run into those guys on the main road. Sarah was hurt bad; she was in a lot of pain and disoriented from being kicked in the head. I decided to make camp on the trail near the lake..."

HD continued to recall as much as he could. Slater realized much of his statement was remarkable in that not only was HD able to survive the night, this kid made it possible for three other people, including a seriously wounded adult, to survive as well. "We had nothing except my hunting knife to defend ourselves, they had guns and even though Ms. Sarah was armed they overtook her, and it all happened so fast. I overheard the conversation between Sarah and that Kyle guy, it sounded as though she held them at gun point right before he shot her."

"Okay HD, sit back and take a deep breath, you're doing good here, uh, we found remains of campfires and fish bones at Bear Lake, I'm interested to know that if everything was at the bottom of the lake, how did you make campfires and catch fish." HD looked away then hung his head, he didn't answer right away.

"Like I said I had my hunting knife with me, strapped to my leg, I wear it for protection."

It didn't dawn on Officer Slater the significance of HD wearing a knife on the school bus let alone to school. HD continued, "Jack had a small box with a couple of fishhooks and a spool of nylon fishing line, I think that day he traded something at school for it. Billy had a yo-yo."

HD continued his statement until his father showed up to take him home. "Thanks HD, that's all for now. I got the rest of the story from Denis, Mark, and the other guys. You can go home today no need to stay here in the hospital."

"Thanks Officer Slater." They shook hands and Slater left HD's room.

"If Sarah would just wake up," Slater said to himself, "I must get an ID on the man in the ICU." Chief Deputy Slater's cell phone rang, "Sir, this is Rudy. Forensics just sent us the vin numbers and license plate from the burned-out truck we picked up this morning. We ran the license, plate, seems its owner is Edward Ringold, of Florida City. Young guy, twenty-two years old, 6 feet 4 inches, light brown hair, blue eyes."

"That may well corroborate what HD Macon told me. He said he remembered one of them was called Eddie. I'm heading to the ICU now."

Slater hung up and made a bee line to the ICU. He approached the triage station and asked one of the nurses, "Where is the John Doe patient that was brought in at dawn, the one with head trauma. The nurse pointed to the end of the hall, "Last room on the right, he's still unconscious as of thirty minutes ago."

Slater called the office and ordered a deputy to come to the hospital to guard Eddie's room. Unlike the other patient rooms, Eddie's room was silent, there were no machines chirping away methodically and the bed was empty. Slater wondered how this guy got away, and desperation crept into his gut. Slater ran down the hall to the triage station, "Where's the John Doe patient, he's not in his room." The nurse checked his chart, and then ran down the hall to check for herself that the patient was gone. The nurse ran back to the triage station and reported the missing patient and said to Slater, "Sir, it appears that he has left without checking out."

"I already know that, and no one saw him leave?"

The other nurses looked at one another, eyes wide, all with the got my hand caught in the cookie jar look on their faces. "Sir, there was no order to restrain or hold that man," the head nurse said defensively. Slater's next thought was maybe he went to Sarah's room,

"Where's Sarah Miller's room?"

"She's down the other end of this hall, room 342," the nurse said.

Slater ran down the hall to Ms. Miller's room, like the other rooms, her machines were beeping and chirping away. She looked like a mummy, all wrapped up in bandages from the ribs up to her shoulders and she was asleep.

Slater searched her room, the closet, and bathroom behind the drapes—no Eddie. He called the office and ordered an APB out on the missing patient and gave the most recent information that he had just acquired. He then called Chief Bowman at the Big Banyan Seminole Reservation for Denis or Mark's cell phone numbers.

"Hey Denis, this is Chief Deputy Slater, seems the John Doe got the slip on us, and left the hospital. I was wondering if you can give us a description of the man, you know, height, age that sort of thing. I know it was pitch black out there on Flamingo Road but do the best you can." Denis paused a second then said, "We pulled him off the truck and I did notice right away that he was a tall man, easily over 6 feet,

and he was young, the fire from the truck lit the
road up enough that I'd say he was a kid, maybe
late teens, early twenties."

CHAPTER 30

Eddie dreamt of cruising down the long bridge to Key West as the balmy ocean air whipped through his hair. He felt so peaceful. Except there's an annoying noise—what's that beep beep sound? Eddie opened his eyes and slowly oriented himself. "I'm in bed," he said as he touched the bed sheets. He touched his chest, and his fingers ran over the hospital gown—he reached up and touched the bandage around his forehead—"oh my head hurts, I hurt myself. — No wait, how long have I been here, and how'd I get here?" he wondered.

He looked at the window; it was daylight. Eddie sat up; both his arms were taped with IV's. "Let me just take this stuff off," he said and ripped off the IV's. Then, Eddie tried to stand up. He blinked through blurry eyes, and his body swerved in dizziness. He looked around with squinty eyes. He stumbled around the room in his hospital gown and wondered where his clothes were.

He staggered over to the closet and found a plastic bag. One of his shoes stuck out of the bag. His hands shook as he dressed in his smokey smelling clothes.

Once dressed, Eddie stumbled around the hospital room, he tried hard to remember—anything. But his mind was so foggy. The only thing that came to mind was the urgency to get out of Florida City. Nauseous, he leaned against the wall and waited for the nausea to pass. Beads of sweat dotted his forehead, and a wave of dizziness passed over him. He clung to a clothing hook on the wall until the nausea passed. Eddie was unaware that his cranium was slowly filling with blood.

"Gotta make it to a stairwell" Eddie muttered as he peeked down the hall, "nothing on the right, and the hall appears to dead end on the left."

He made his way to the stairwell and down three flights of stairs. At the entrance to the hospital, Eddie hailed a taxi, "Florida City Bus Station," he told the driver. His eyes blurred and another wave of dizziness and nausea overwhelmed him.

When he arrived at the bus station Eddie pulled out a crumpled twenty-dollar bill from his pocket and gave it to the taxi driver. He staggered into the bus station, collapsed onto a bench, and had forgotten why he came to the station. After a few moments, he remembered that he had a locker here where he had stored some of his things for safekeeping—and until he was ready to leave town. The locker number was in the third row, somewhere in the middle, number 8, the number of his birthday month.

"What's the combination?" Eddie said to himself, hindered by dizziness and nausea. "Oh, yea it's in my wallet, it's tucked in my wallet. I remember now, it's scribbled on a piece of paper."

But the only thing in Eddie's pockets now was a few dollars change leftover from the taxi, "My wallet's gone! Okay, I can do this, just gotta calm down and think—if this dizziness would just go away," Eddie moaned.

He sat down on a bus bench. This time, in the middle of the row of rented lockers, he waited for the dizzy spell to pass; took slow deep breaths and calmed himself.

"I remember now, it's 10-05-19, the day dad died. Yea that's it," he said and opened his locker. Everything he needed was right there, in a backpack; a new wallet, not one but three credit cards, his license, passport, money and a change of clothes.

"Dad," Eddie said aloud, "you taught me to be prepared, always be prepared for anything, always have a backup plan." To the memory of his father Eddie continued, "I didn't kill anyone, I know you're not happy that I robbed that bank, and that woman, she wasn't ever part of the plan, but there she was, drove up next to us, and I had nothing to do with her dying. I didn't kill her, and I didn't want her to die. I don't kill people. I'm in a mess Dad, but I'm getting out of this mess and I'm never ever going to screw up again," he said between silent sobs.

Eddie threw the backpack over his shoulder and headed for the bathroom where he changed clothes. He vomited twice, his eyes blurred, and a splitting headache gripped him. His knees buckled, and he collapsed to the urine-stained floor. He pulled himself up and leaned against the bathroom wall and waited for the pain to pass.

Finally, the waves of pain and blurring vision subsided. He went to the ticket counter and bought a ticket to Key West. The bus was scheduled to arrive in an hour, "I have an hour, so I'll just sit here, and hope this dizziness goes away," Eddie said to himself.

In the waiting area, there was a vending machine, with band-aids, aspirins, pins—the little things needed when traveling. Eddie bought 4 packets of aspirin. "This will take care of the headache, let's see 4 pills in a pack, that's 16 pills. I'll just swallow the aspirin down with a soda, yea, that should take care of it," Eddie assured himself.

After a fashion, the headache began to dim, but he was still groggy and wondered if he might have taken one too many aspirins. The feeling of nausea was ever present now and while he felt the need to vomit his stomach was empty. The dizziness was worse than ever too.

Eddie's heartbeat pumped into high gear, his hands shook, and waves of convulsions overwhelmed him. Eddie endured it all until the hallucinations started. "What are you doing here?" Eddie exclaimed.

Kyle and Ben looked down at Eddie. They each had a smirk on their faces. Kyle nodded, Eddie knew what it meant, "Yea I'm getting away, got that Kyle? The mess you caused us— I'm getting away. You can stand here and grin all you want, but when that bus pulls out, I'll be on it. You? Dead. You too Ben. I pulled you out of the water, remember? Set you in your car, there you two were, Kyle dead as door nail, and you Ben, can't be sure whether you're dead or not. But there you two were just sitting in your cars. The money? I left it, at the Visitor Center for the cops to find, yea, I didn't take a dime of it, that's right you're dead and I'm not, and there is nothing you can do about it!"

Eddie slumped over on the bench and dozed. He was startled awake when the loudspeaker announced the boarding call for Key West. Another wave of dizziness and nausea swept over him as he grabbed his backpack, pulled out his ticket and got in line. He tried to ignore the nausea and dizziness, "Just focus—that's it, just get in line, three ahead of me now, I'm almost next."

"Ticket please."

"Here you go," Eddie said. His hand trembled as he gave the ticket to the attendant. He took a seat at the back of the half empty bus. A flashback of the sinking yellow school bus washed over him, and he wondered if the fish found the woman Kyle killed. He wondered if the fish ate her up, maybe a gator got her. "Guess I'll never know."

Once the bus was underway, a thin stream of cool air rushed out of the air conditioning vents above the passengers. The ride was smooth, and the bus hummed down the road. Eddie set his backpack on the empty seat next to him. He felt secure in the half-full bus. A deep sense of calm slowly passed over him. He leaned his head back on the head rest and thought of Kyle and Ben.

A small child from across the aisle looked at Eddie and smiled but Eddie didn't smile back, he just stared back at her with unblinking eyes.

"Mommy, that man is staring at me," the little girl whined. The child's mother turned to look at the man whose eyes were in a fixed stare, his face drained of all color. The child's mother knew he was dead. "Not my problem," the woman said, and she and her daughter got up and quietly changed seats.

The bus stopped at Sims Diner halfway to Key West. After all the passengers got off the bus the driver walked the length of the bus to be sure no one was left behind before he locked the bus doors. He wondered how long the man in seat number 54 had been dead. He dreaded the call to the authorities, "What a miserable deal," the driver moaned, "a dead body on my watch, now the bus will be late getting to the Key West terminal."

CHAPTER 31

I was totally disoriented when I woke up.

"How long have I been in the hospital?"

"Ms. Miller you've been here a week," the ICU nurse said.

"Why am I here?"

"Well, you've suffered a gunshot wound and a concussion. The concussion requires strict bed rest."

"I see, and when will I be discharged?"

"I'll call your doctor, and he will talk to you about a discharge, okay?"

I nodded and the nurse smiled back at me then left my room. I had been dreaming about three children who ride my bus every day and a camp out at Bear Lake. In the dream we were not afraid. It was a pleasant time for all of us and, the school children were my children, and I loved them.

Every now and then, somewhere in the back of my mind I felt haunted by a sense of trouble. Something was not right. The idyllic camping dream turned bittersweet and was not going to have a happy ending—not for me. I felt as though something was coming for me. Trouble brewed in the back of my mind. Trouble that would not have occurred if I had done things differently. I made a big mistake.

My dream had taken a turn, a sense of dread darkened the joy I felt camping with the boys at the idyllic Bear Lake. I made a big mistake, but I couldn't figure it out in my dream state. Then, I woke up and pain consumed me. I'm not a crybaby and generally don't feel sorry for myself yet here I am crying my eyes out.

Every breath was a gasp and cough that shot pain through my chest and face. My right eye was swollen. I saw things I did not recognize through blurry eyes. My head throbbed.

How long did the nurse say I've been here? This—hospital. I looked at my hands, a tremor owned them. Hot tears roll down my bruised cheeks and my face ached at the thought of moving. I felt beaten up.

The floor nurse returned and said, "Hey Ms. Miller, I've brought some pain medicine for you. I know you're hurtin'."

The nurse took her stethoscope from around her neck and took my blood pressure. Minutes later a doctor walked into my room. After a few pleasantries, the doctor said, "You've been through a terrible ordeal, and it is normal for you to feel frightened and disoriented upon waking. You had a serious infection in your wound which over the past week has improved immensely. Your bruises—will fade, and the swelling has gone down. With continued rest at home, you should have full recovery from the concussion you suffered. However, it will take some time and rest is essential. We are glad to see you're sitting up."

The doctor paused a second and then said softly, "The worst is over for you, I have several medications you need to take, and I will have the nurse prepare them for you. You are free to go, however, you must have continued bed rest for the next several weeks."

I got the gist of most everything he said, especially the part about going home, "Do you have someone to take you home?" I smiled back at him through my tears and nodded. But there was no one in my life to care for me anymore.

After he left, the nurse returned, "There's a man that's checked on you every day since you got here. Chief Deputy Slater, do you know him? He's a great guy he wants to talk to you but not until you are ready to see him," the nurse said as she removed the IV needles from my arm and reassuringly handed me two pills and a small cup of water. "These meds are for pain," she said as she handed me a small paper cup with two small white pills, "for patients who have suffered such a trauma as yours."

I took the pills and waited for them to take effect. It wasn't long before I felt my body relax. The nurse gently removed the bandage on my chest and replaced it with a clean one. Then, she sponge-bathed me and washed my hair with some odd shampoo that's inside a fitted shower cap of sorts.

After the in-the-cap shampoo, the nurse pulled a clean hospital gown over my head and ran a comb through my hair. She got me up out of bed and walked me over to a chair where I stayed until she changed the bed sheets. When I got back in bed the full effect of the pain killers hit me. I felt as though I had entered heaven.

I closed my eyes. I didn't have a care in the world. I was relieved to be out of pain and worry free. I figured now's a good time to call a taxi. So I removed the hospital gown and dressed myself. I was confident I could slip out of the hospital unseen. While I continued to mentally plot my disappearance from the hospital, a man walked into my room. He was at least a foot taller than me. He held a deputy hat in his hand and there was a chief deputy badge in full display upon his chest.

CHAPTER 32

When Chief Deputy Slater got back to the Office, an APB on Edward Ringold had been issued. At the same time, the bus company called the police, who had Eddie's body transported to the Monroe County morgue. Slater couldn't believe his luck, "The man makes a run for it and dies in the process," he said to himself, "It's incredulous, that three college grads rob a bank, hijack a bus with its driver and three school kids. Now, those college grads are dead and lying in the morgue."

The nurse at the triage desk buzzed Slater's cell phone, "Hello Officer Slater, you asked me to call you when Ms. Miller is awake. Also, her doctor would like to speak to you."

The nurse handed the phone to Sarah's doctor, "Officer Slater, this is Doctor Gomez. Ms. Miller's awake and alert and we are treating her for trauma as well as a gunshot wound, concussion, and facial bruises. She is physically weak but, as I said before, she is alert and can go home. She may be a bit woozy when you get here."

"I'll be right over."

Slater needed to get his thoughts together before he headed over to the hospital. He had many questions to ask Ms. Miller—beginning with who shot who. He was sure her statements on everything else would corroborate with Billy, HD, and Jack's statements as well as the Big Banyan trail runners. Slater looked out the glass partition between his office and the main floor. There were what appeared to be angry people in conversation with one of the deputies. The deputy appeared to be in distress.

The deputy turned and walked to Slater's office. "What's up with the crowd?" Slater asked.

"We have an attorney, several people from the school board and some people from the bank."

"Tell the bank folks to make an appointment. What does the school board people want?"

"They want to press charges against Sarah Miller, for violation of the school transport regulations regarding the stop at the side of the road. Seems she broke some rule by picking up those hijackers."

"What does the attorney want?"

"Well Sir, he represents parents of the children who were on the bus, they want to sue the school and press charges against Ms. Miller for child endangerment."

"Tell them all to make an appointment, I'm leaving now to see Ms. Miller. No need to say anything to the crowd as to her whereabouts. You have no information, about her, we clear?"

"Yes sir."

Slater slipped out the side door of his office that faced the parking lot, intent on getting to the hospital before one of his officers got there with an arrest warrant for Ms. Miller. When Slater arrived, Sarah was dressed and sitting in a chair. A large bandage peeked out of Sarah's blood-stained shirt.

Slater took notice of her slender, muscular body. She reminded him of the 5K runners that he often saw running aside the road. Her face was gaunt and swollen with black and blue contusions. One eye was puffy.

Without introducing himself, Slater asked, "When can you go home?"

"The doctor said today," Sarah waved her discharge papers, "I'm waiting for my taxi,"

"Ms. Miller, I'm Chief Deputy Slater with the Florida City Sheriff's department. I've been coming by regularly to check on you—to see how you're coming along," Slater felt a little sheepish with his introduction.

"Oh, yes, the nurse just told me that you've been dropping by. I've been out of it for a few days."

"Yes, that's true. Do you have anyone to help you out at home?" Sarah looked at him through sad weary eyes, "I live alone Officer Slater, my husband died in Afghanistan several years ago. I plan to slip out of here and take a taxi home just as soon as you leave."

"I'm sorry about your husband." Slater already knew her history all her information was made available days ago when she disappeared with the bus. She's a veteran, an American hero who engaged in combat—and a widow. Her army discharge was honorable and distinguished.

"I'll take you home, today."

"Okay, I appreciate that."

I pondered the invitation. I guess it won't be a problem if I ride with a deputy. I just want to go home, plus, what choice do I have, there's no one else and the ride is free, I hope.

Chief Deputy Slater nodded and almost laughed aloud probably at my dopey smile.

"Okay let's do this."

Slater moved quickly to get me out of the hospital as fast as he could. "Ms. Miller, I need to talk to you before anyone else does. As a law enforcement officer, I'm walking the line, but with all you've been through, saving Billy, the return of all the bank money, finding the bus, and the soon to be three bodies in the morgue, I have a problem with you being charged with criminal acts. As we speak, there is an arrest warrant out on you that I'm going to sidestep for now. Where do you live Ms. Miller?"

"I'm a few blocks from The County School Bus Barn."

I gave Slater my address. Aside from my injuries now I have to worry about getting arrested. He could get in a lot of trouble doing this, helping a soon to be fugitive to avoid arrest. But for some reason I'm glad he's looking out for me, it's the right thing to do, even if he's about to lose his rank and pension.

Slater helped me into a wheelchair, covered me up with a white cotton blanket and wheeled me down the busy corridor past the triage desk and into the elevator. But once he was outside, instead of using the valet, he continued through the parking lot to the law enforcement slot up front near the ER where his car was parked.

***

Within minutes, Slater knew that his deputies would be knocking on Sarah's hospital room door to issue an arrest warrant. Sure enough, one of his deputies called, "Sir, we have a warrant for Sarah Miller. We're at her room, apparently, she left before checking out and no one here noticed her leaving."

"Check her house." Slater said. He had no intention of taking her to her home, rather he was taking her to his place until he unraveled all the facts. Slater drove past the road to her home, and five miles later he turned off the Tamiami Trail and into a subdivision. His house was conveniently hidden by a row of shrubs and palm trees. He lived alone. His wife gave up competing with his work and divorced him five years ago. He'd been consumed with his work ever since. Lately, Slater found himself lonely and bored. At least until the bank got robbed and the bus got stolen.

CHAPTER 33

"What are you doing," I asked, gripped with panic, my eyes filled with tears, I am helpless to fight or struggle with anyone. I'm terrified.

Slater pulled into a driveway and drove into the garage and closed the garage door. He looked over at me. I glared an angry look at him. Slater turned and faced me, "Okay Ms. Miller, here's what's going down. Some of the parents want you arrested for child endangerment. I ah, well—I think the demands of the children's parents via their lawyers are a little premature. I have testimony from HD, Billy, and Jack as well as the trail runners and their statements corroborate. I need you to ID the three bodies in the morgue and, after that, I want to know what happened out there on Tamiami Trail as you remember it. I invite you to stay here until my deputies are no longer knocking on your door to arrest you."

"Arrest me! For what?"

"Lawyers for the kids and the school system say you pulled over, opened the bus doors and let hijackers into the bus, with three kids inside, to open the bus doors to anyone except the children is against regulations," Slater said in a sad tone of voice, "you violated a transport policy and as a result, three men are dead, and three kids are traumatized—need I say more?"

"I knew it, I dreamt something was wrong, I couldn't put my finger on it, but I woke up in a panic this morning, what you just said—that's it. I didn't pull over to the side of the road, I was at a stop light at the Tamiami Stop & Shop. I was *forced* to open the bus doors at gunpoint."

I put my hands over my bruised face and began to weep. I am frustrated and humiliated at my helplessness and now a fugitive from the law. I'm overwhelmed.

Slater winced at Sarah's tears, "Let's go in the house and get you squared away. Believe me, no one is coming near you until you are on your feet and can speak clearly about what happened. In the meantime, I intend to meet with the three boys that were in the bus. I might even bring them over here. I know they're concerned about you."

****

After Slater got Sarah settled in, he went back to the office. Deputy Rudy Pepper was waiting for him, warrant in hand.

"We have a warrant for the arrest of Sarah Miller, according to Mr. Bilford Lorring, Attorney at Law, there's a lawsuit against the County of Monroe and Ms. Sarah Miller for child endangerment. The lawyer represents Mr. and Mrs. William Culpepper, parents of Billy Culpepper and Ms. Mildred Weller, mother of Jack Weller. These parents want her arrested and prosecuted. We went out to her house, but no one's there, and of course we checked the hospital first, but she'd left without official discharge."

"It's not a crime to walk out of a hospital now, is it?" Slater asked.

"She's missing, sir," Deputy Pepper insisted, "she must have known we were coming."

"Look for her, that's all I can say." Slater knew there was no lie in saying look for her and was confident his deputies had no intention of looking for her at his place.

The local news station broadcasted the sensational story of the missing children, bus driver and bank robbery and it made national headlines. Attorney Lorring was televised with both sets of parents standing behind him. He spoke on their behalf,

"Ms. Miller is a resident of Florida City and a veteran who may be suffering from PTSD. If so, why did the school system hire such a person to drive helpless innocent children? On behalf of the parents of these poor children, a lawsuit is being filed against the school system and Ms. Miller. In addition, Ms. Miller is being charged with child endangerment. An arrest warrant has been issued. I intend to convict this woman of child endangerment and put her behind bars where she can never put another child in harms' way, " Attorney Lorring promised.

"I instantly dislike this guy," Slater mumbled to himself, "his speech smacks of sensational opportunism. Obviously, there were no details about the incident, or this would have never happened."

Nothing was said about how the victims survived with a knife, fish hooks, and a spool of fishing line, or the courage of the bus driver as she tried to protect the kids by saying she was the only one on the bus, or how she had been forced to surrender the bus at gun point and never intended to get out of the bus, or turn the bus off, and how the thugs entered the bus and forced Sarah out onto the side of the road and threw her down in the dirt.

Nothing was said about how she bravely stood her ground and held them at gunpoint in self-defense of herself and the children. Nothing was said about how she was at a stop light on the highway, and that was the only reason the bus had stopped. In Slater's opinion, she did nothing wrong, she never turned the bus off. Sarah was forced from the drivers' seat at gunpoint.

Lorring said nothing about Sarah being shot or beaten and thrown down the aisle of the bus for dead. Hadn't she had enough? The lawyer thinks he has all the facts, "What a fool," Slater said to no one… "I have no intention of giving Sarah up. Lorring will have a lot of explaining to do. All the facts will be revealed when I give a public statement. For now, I need to sidestep and give Deputy Pepper a brief statement to read to the press."

Slater called the Sheriff, "I'm requesting a week off, Sir. This is a tough case, and more information is coming in that will continue to linger in the press. This has been a 24/7 case, and I need a break."

Headquarters granted him time off. On the way home from the station, Slater stopped by a remote drug store a good distance from Florida City. No one recognized him or the name on Sarah's prescriptions either. In addition to the prescription medicine Slater purchased bandages and over the counter anti-bacterial ointments. He hoped the cashier hadn't been listening to the news. Usually, an infomercial or one of those inane morning shows for the customers waiting for their prescriptions was on in the store, rarely was there any news.

Slater finished at the drug store, then drove out to a discount clothing store. He guessed Sarah's size, purchased some clothes he thought would fit her; a set of PJs, jeans, sweats, a couple of pairs of summer shorts and t-shirts and some underwear for a size small woman.

"Why do I feel a little embarrassed? I was married once upon a time. This shouldn't make me feel awkward, but I am," Slater thought to himself as he approached the cashier. She rung up the clothes without missing a beat.

Sarah was asleep when he got home. He placed the bags of clothes on a chair by her bed. Slater was confident that when she woke up, she'd notice the duds were for her.

***

It was late afternoon when I woke up. I stepped outside to the back patio. Slater had several steaks on his gas grill. A platter was in one hand and a BBQ fork in the other.

"Hey," I say.

"I'm getting ready to start some dinner, you slept all day, are you hungry?"

"I'm in pain, Officer, I need some pain meds."

"I took the liberty of picking up your prescriptions and—well I see you've found the clothes."

"Yes, thank you, I'll pay you back soon as I get on my feet."

I followed deputy chief Slater back to the kitchen. I noticed how he checked out my outfit. The clothes were a little too big, but I didn't care. "You're a bit more petite than I realized," Slater said as he put out Sarah's meds for her. "Here you go. I've taken the liberty of putting your medications out," Slater said as he showed me two bottles of pills.

"I've read the instructions for the type of care you need for that chest wound, says it should be tended to everyday for another week, Slater said, "I can help you with that."

"Thanks."

"How 'bout a cup of coffee?"

"How 'bout a glass of wine?"

Slater cocked his head to one side, and I knew what he was thinking. Maybe I need to wait until I'm done with the meds. Then he reminded me, "I'm pretty sure the meds have warnings on them to not mix with alcohol."

"Oh, yes, of course, where are the meds?"

"Here you go."

Slater handed me two pills and a glass of water. I swallowed them down in two gulps.

I've got no appetite. I was preoccupied with getting rid of the concussion headache that's plagued me since I woke up in the hospital. I looked at the grilled steaks and knew the next question would be *I hope you're hungry.* So, I said, "I'm not hungry yet, the steaks look great, but I just want to go back to my room."

Slater was visibly disappointed, but I just wasn't back to normal yet.

***

Slater looked down at the bottle of pills, the directions on the bottle of oxycontin said take two pills every 12 hours, that meant Sarah was going to be up at 4 o'clock in the morning for her next dose—or earlier. "Tonight, I'll sleep with pill bottles in my pockets," Slater thought to himself, disappointed that he will be eating alone tonight.

***

When I saw myself in the bathroom mirror, I was shocked to see my beat up, scared to death

248

self. I put on the new clothes Slater got for me and was determined to present myself alert and strong. Well, maybe I could present myself alert but I'm too bruised up to appear strong.

The next day Slater decided to take me over to the morgue to ID the bodies of the three men who hijacked the bus. He could tell I tried to put on a courageous 'face' and, he knew a façade when he saw one, my facial expressions gave me away, and I was scared six ways to Sunday.

CHAPTER 34

With Sarah being so frail and wounded, Slater wondered how long she'd last in the Florida heat. He planned to make the ID as quick and painless as possible then get her back to the house before anyone recognized her or God forbid, she passed out. Slater called the morgue and talked to his old buddy Dr. Matt Fry, the county morgue pathologist, a man who has had Slater's back for twenty years.

"I'll have the bodies ready to view when you walk in the door," Dr. Fry said, "make it quick, family members have been calling asking when the funeral home can pick up their loved ones remains for burial. They're getting a little edgy, wondering why we are holding them so long."

"Who are the families?"

"The family of Kyle Moleto," Dr. Fry said, "and the sister of Ben Sykes, Peggy Sue, I went to high school with her."

"I know that name," Slater said, "Sykes—nice family, good reputation in the neighborhood. Do you know what she does for a living—whether she's married?"

"Truth is, Slater, Peggy Sue Sykes never married, she works over at the digital Securities Center that monitors the video intake for the Department of School Transportation. You know, the videos they put in the buses to record the behavior of the kids and drivers."

"So, Peggy Sue Sykes is Ben Sykes sister— hmm."

"Actually, his older sister, and the word is she put him through college."

"See you around mid-morning to ID the bodies, thanks Matt."

Slater made a mental note to inquire about the bus's video box and whether it has been recovered from the bus yet.

***

When we arrived at the morgue, Dr. Fry had prepared the corpses of the three young men for viewing. He pulled the corpse shroud down on each body long enough for me to ID the men. I tried hard not to lose it or pass out. "You alright Sarah, your face is white as a sheet?"

"Yea I'm alright," I said as I pointed to one of the men, "he held me at gunpoint and demanded entry into the bus. It was in broad daylight, right there at the traffic light across from the Tamiami Stop & Shop. I had no choice but to open the doors. He cocked the handgun. I couldn't take the chance of him killing me *and* the children," my eyes welled with tears, but I continued, "before I opened the doors, I shouted out to the children to get down and hide and they did, under the circumstances it was all I could do. I hated having to open the bus doors. Then, when I did open the doors, this man," I pointed to Kyle Moleto's corpse, "this one told me to move to another seat and took over the driver's seat and that's when the two other men entered the bus. He turned the bus onto Flamingo Road and drove about a mile or so from the main highway. He pulled over and told me to get off the bus, which I did. He wanted to use my cell phone, and I wouldn't give it to him. We argued. I wanted to make a call for them, but he insisted and when I wouldn't give him the phone, he pulled his gun on me. I made a run for the bus, but he pulled me back and threw me down on the ground. I rolled a couple of times and managed to pull my revolver from my back holster, to defend myself. I remember they all backed down or so it seemed, I should have held them at gun point, gotten back on the bus and driven away with them in my gun site. But they started talking sense and I let my guard down and lowered my gun that's when this guy," Sarah pointed to Kyle, "shot me. He kicked my gun out of my hand, and he kept kicking me…I don't remember anything after that until I saw Jack's face looking at me from under one of the bus seats. I remember when HD pulled me to the back of the bus. It's a wonder we all didn't get killed. Then, HD orchestrated the escape out the back of the bus."

"Okay," Slater said softly, "let's go to body number two."

I recognized the corpse immediately, "This man laughed when Kyle shot me, and because I recognized his voice at the Marina, I believe this is the man I shot."

"You're sure it was him you shot?"

"Yes, the loud laughter, he had a very threatening, maniacal voice tone. One you never forget, full of meanness and cold." Slater looked at me, I knew he felt sorry for me.

"Why did you shoot him?"

"Billy turned the lights on in the Marina store where we were hiding. He didn't mean to light up the whole store. He was trying to get power to the phone jacks, but the place lit up like a Christmas tree, the music went on and blared out through the bull horns. I hollered at him to turn them off and he did, but it was too late they heard the music and saw the lights."
I felt myself losing control as terror crept over me. "Take your time," Slater said.

"What I'm about to say recurs in nightmares. I don't know how many days I was in the hospital but be sure of this, I dreamt constantly of Billy peeking out a window and seeing two men arguing. One of them says don't go over there, we gotta get outta here, and the other man persisted on checking out the Marina, he knew it was me hiding in the Marina. So, he made his way over to us real slow like. God, he taunted us with a sing song whispery voice, it was so creepy. I told Billy to hide under the desk in the office, which he did, but he was terrified. He

254

cried and whimpered loud enough for the man to hear him. I had maneuvered myself behind some boxes against the back wall, armed with one of the trail runner's hunting rifles. Denis insisted I have it just in case I needed to defend myself and Billy. It was dark but I could tell the man was coming closer and closer, because he kept singing that sick tune. Billy was near hysterical. He must have covered his mouth because his cries were muffled but still loud enough for the man to hear him. I could see the outline of the man's body as he stood at the door of the office. He fired his gun twice, but it misfired both times. Then, I hollered at him to leave, I didn't want to kill him. I heard his feet shuffle my way. He fired a third time in my direction, again the gun misfired and before he could pull the trigger a fourth time, I shot him. He was thrown halfway up the aisle and stumbled out the door. I heard a splash and then I must have blacked out. The next thing I knew, Billy and I were being picked up and put in the helicopter. That's it, that's all I remember."

"Slater," interrupted Dr. Fry, "we need to conclude these identifications, the families have the funeral homes coming out in another hour to pick them up."

"Okay," Slater said, "one more body then, we're done."

I looked at Eddie a little longer than the other two, then I said, "He didn't do anything to stop the hijacking of the bus. He told the other two guys that hijacking a bus and shooting the bus driver wasn't part of the plan, they argued amongst themselves. I remember his voice," Sarah pointed to Ben, "these two argued at the Marina, yea, this is the third man that boarded my bus at gunpoint and hijacked it and kidnapped me and the boys."

"We're done here, Matt."

Slater gently led me back to the car and drove me back to his house, helped me back to my room and made sure that I was comfortable before he said, "I must get to the office, but I'll be back later today, don't answer the door to anyone." I nodded to Slater and shut my eyes as he pulled the bedroom door closed.

***

Slater drove back to the office and was about to call Forensics when he got a call from Deputy Hillert, "Sir, we have the forensics report and information about the school bus video cams, it appears that the videos above the rearview mirror in the front of the bus and the back of the bus above the exit doors are permanently damaged and show no video feed at all."

"Thanks, Hillert, I am on my way to the School Securities building to check out the video feed on Bus 51 the day it was hijacked."

Slater wondered why nothing had been said about the video before now. In fact, he wondered why it wasn't called in the day the bus disappeared. "Sounds like a terrific oversight," Slater mused.

CHAPTER 35

Peggy Sue Sykes sat in her bedroom with the drapes pulled shut. She called her office and left a message for her boss, "Hello, this Peggy Sue, my brother died, and I need a few family days. Thanks."

The pathologist at the morgue called a few minutes later but Peggy Sue let the call go to voicemail, "Ms. Sykes, this is Dr. Fry with the Florida City morgue, we are releasing Ben's body to the funeral home you requested, and they will be out to pick up his body this afternoon."

Peggy Sue went to her desk and made two phone calls; the first to her pastor who agreed to preside over a brief graveside service at the cemetery, and the second to secure the purchase of two cemetery plots next to where her parents were buried. She read over her handwritten to do list and put a check mark next to each task completed.

Peggy Sue recalled the day bus 51 went missing. She just happened to be monitoring the buses that day. She did the right thing by her brother and had taken the video of the bus and hid it amongst her things. She had been tempted to substitute a previous recording of the bus activities and alter the video date but for some reason she chose not to do that. She was afraid someone might catch her substituting the video. She pulled out the video and went to her flat screen TV one more time and turned it on.

Peggy Sue watched as the bus drove down Tamiami Trail and routinely dropped off the school children. It was a typical routine without event until it got to the traffic light across from the Tamiami Stop & Shop.

The large gas station on the left of the screen was clearly visible. She knew exactly where they were. She watched as Sarah pulled up at the light with three children randomly located in the bus. Suddenly, Ms. Miller turned towards the doors, then looked away, then looked back. Peggy Sue clearly heard Sarah say, *"No, I can't let you in."* Peggy Sue watched and listened as Sarah looked away and said as loud as she could, *"Children get down and hide."* Then, one of the kids ran up the aisle and before Sarah opened the bus doors, he grabbed two younger boys and dragged them to the back of the bus.

The exit door video showed them hiding behind the last set of seats.

Peggy Sue watched as Sarah Miller put her hands up, palms out and said, *"Okay."* She watched as Sarah opened the bus doors. A man entered the bus and pointed a gun at Sarah and shouted at her to get out of the driver's seat then he took over the bus. Two other guys climbed into the bus behind him.

Peggy Sue paused the video feed, stared at the screen and wept, "Ben." There was no mistaking that one of the hijackers was her brother Ben. She forced herself to push the play button and continued watching the video.

She watched as the man who took over the bus turned right and onto Flamingo Road. He then stopped a short distance up the road. He forced Sarah at gun point out of the bus. The video did not show what went down outside the bus. However, the audio picked up the sound of a gunshot and loud voices arguing. It picked up Ben's voice, loud, angry and aggressive. Peggy Sue paused the video again. She was overcome and sick to her stomach and felt as though she was going to vomit.

After a few moments, she pressed the play button and continued watching as the three men got back in the bus. Ben and the man with the gun dragged Sarah down the middle of the bus and dropped her in the center aisle. The bus driver was covered in blood and, appeared dead. Peggy Sue paused the video again and reached for a cigarette, her hands trembled as she lit a match. She took two long drags on the cigarette, exhaled, poured a second glass of bourbon and drank it down.

She pushed the video play button and watched Ben's buddy drive the bus back onto Tamiami Trail. He made a U-turn onto the highway and came around behind a jeep along the soft shoulder and pulled up behind the vehicle. This time the three men unloaded large bags from the spare tire well of the jeep and threw then down the aisle of the bus. Peggy Sue counted six bags. A bank logo was printed on the side of each bag.

"So, my precious brother, you were also involved with the bank robbery that's been plastered all over the news," Peggy Sue said in an intoxicated drawl. She listened intently to a conversation amongst the three men about a hideout. "How could I have missed seeing this cold, calculating side to my baby brother. This video doesn't lie, it sure looks and sounds like you, Ben, how could you do this," Peggy Sue said between drunken sobs.

Ben was fourteen years old when their parents died in a car crash. At the time, Peggy Sue was twenty-one years old and awarded legal guardianship of Ben. "I raised you up Ben, only because it was unthinkable for me to put you in a foster home. There was no need—you were a good kid, and I cared for you as though you were my own son."

Peggy Sue recalled the money she saved for Ben's college fund and the parishioners who worked tirelessly to raise additional funds to send one of their own to a prestigious college. "You were my pride and joy, Ben, the jewel in my crown, a rising star in the community, soon to be a licensed contractor," Peggy Sue stuttered between sobs, "I just spoke with you earlier this week and as usual, there was not even an inkling of untoward nastiness in you, Ben."

Peggy Sue continued the punishing viewing of her brother's activities as his buddy drove the bus south on Flamingo Road. She fast forwarded to when they arrived in front of the old Visitor Center across from the Flamingo Marina. She watched as each man picked up a couple of bags and carried them out of the bus and out of the video's focus.

Two of the children appeared in the video, hunched over, their voices were too low to understand. Together they dragged the bus driver to the back of the bus and hid her with them.

This was the fifteenth time Peggy Sue watched the video to the very end. Right up until the bus sank to the bottom of Bear Lake. It never changed, no matter how many times Peggy Sue watched the video, it always ended the same way. She had watched the video over and over until her eyes burned. Robbery, hijacking, accessory to a possible murder and now her baby brother is dead—Peggy Sue was devastated. Very soon the whole community will know that Peggy Sue's younger brother was involved in these heinous crimes.

She had taken the video from the security system's recorder, to give her more time to prepare for the inevitable. Of course, video feed for bus 51 was now missing. The authorities could only see the fuzzy grey screen when they attempted to bring up the video at her monitoring station.

Very soon the authorities will come knocking at Peggy Sue's door. She wanted to do the right thing, but the humiliation was beyond the pale of comprehension. This thing Ben did, was a mortifying death knell for Peggy Sue on so many levels. Ben brought such shame and despondency to his sister.

Peggy Sue cried out to her parents, "Thank God you are no longer with us, gone and, in heaven, you would never have survived the shock of it all."

Peggy Sue wiped away her tears and tended to some paperwork. She prepared a letter to the Pastor of her church with a courtesy stipend check of $50 for the service at the cemetery for Ben. In addition, she wrote a check and addressed an envelope to the funeral home for Ben's funeral expenses. In another envelope, she put a cashier's check for the sum of Peggy Sue's life savings, together with the deed to her house and a letter addressed to the pastor that documented accurately every penny the church raised for Ben's college tuition. Peggy Sue stamped the envelopes, put them in the mailbox and set the metal, red flag up to alert the postman to pick up the out-going mail.

The next morning, Peggy Sue woke up feeling good. She dressed for the day and drove down to her hair salon and spa. In addition to having a facial, she had her hair washed and set, then treated herself to a manicure. She looked great, everyone at the salon said so too.

Finally, she dined at the restaurant where the tables were set with crisp linen tablecloths and vases of fresh flowers in the center of each table. She ordered baked red snapper, salad, and a baked potato with sour cream. While not a connoisseur of wine, still, Peggy Sue ordered two glasses of the most expensive wine the restaurant carried. To top it off, she completed her meal with her favorite dessert, key lime pie and fresh coffee.

Peggy Sue enjoyed the wonderful outing and smiled all the way home. Upon entering her home, Peggy Sue deliberately left the front door open as a warm welcome to anyone that might come calling. She was confident one or two officers from the sheriff's office would be visiting very soon.

She showered and dressed in the flamingo pink summer dress and bolero top that she wore to Ben's graduation. She looked at herself in the mirror and smiled. "Everything is going to be just fine," she told herself.

Then, she placed the bus 51 video she took from her office and placed it in a manila envelope. She addressed it to Officer Lou Slater and set it in plain sight on her vanity table. She pulled out a handgun from a dresser drawer and made sure it was loaded. She then set the gun down next to the manila envelope.

Peggy Sue looked at herself in the mirror one last time and smiled at her reflection, "I did everything right Mama, I'm at peace and I know it's time to join you and Daddy."

****

The postman drove up to Peggy Sue's house and picked up the outgoing mail. As he pulled away from the house, he thought he heard a passing car backfire. He looked out the rear-view mirror and thought it was apparently not a problem, as the car had driven out of sight.

CHAPTER 36

"Good morning, Officer Slater so good to see you!" Mary Louise Pettigrew said, as she greeted Slater with a smile wide on her face. A little tag on her blouse made it clear to anyone that she was the associate in charge of Digital Security Systems. "How can I help you today?"

"I'm here to check the video monitors for bus 51," Slater said, confident that the video was missing.

Ms. Pettigrew went through the motions of looking for the video, but after a fashion she finally turned to Slater with a tremor in her voice and admitted, "I've been searching everywhere for the video Officer Slater, and we can't find it anywhere."

"When did you notice the video was missing?"

"The very day the bus went missing, my supervisor, Ms. Sykes checked the monitor immediately and said that the system was experiencing some malfunction, and that there was no video feed coming from bus 51. But I checked all the monitors that morning, it's my job to see that they're on and recording. I know that the system was on and working otherwise all the monitors would have been down."

"I see, well keep looking I'm sure it will show up."

Slater already knew the answer to why the video was missing, and he knew where to go next. Paying a visit to a relative of someone like Ben Sykes was not going to be easy. It never bodes well to pay a visit to good hard-working, upstanding members of a community that bear the burden and stigma of a criminal family member.

When Slater arrived at Peggy Sue's house, he immediately noticed that the front door was ajar. He knocked on the door, "Anyone home?" He called out again then entered a few feet into the house, hat in hand. The house was clean and in impeccable order. Family pictures were laid out neatly on tables and walls. He continued to call out to Ms. Sykes but still no answer. Slater searched room to room until he came upon Peggy Sue's body, arched back against a chair in front of a vanity table.

Slater winced at the thought of someone killing themselves in front of a mirror. Her body was still warm. Slater called in what appeared to be a suicide. He noticed a manila envelope on the vanity table with his name on it neatly propped up on the front of vanity mirror. He opened the envelope and removed a video with a label taped to the video jacket; "Bus 51 hijacking." Slater waited until the forensic team arrived before he headed back to the office with video in hand.

He was supposed to be on leave for a few days, so the deputies were a bit surprised to see him in his office watching a video. Slater nodded to his deputies and said, "Take a seat, boys."

Together with his deputies, they watched the video in silence. Everything the kids on the bus said was true and everything Sarah said was true. "This is everything we need to show the press and that arrogant SOB lawyer, Mr. Bilford Lorring, to prove them wrong and vindicate Sarah Miller. Now, we have every reason to believe that Ms. Miller shot Ben Sykes in self-defense, even though Billy was the only 'ear' witness of the shooting at the Marina."

Slater called a press conference. Surrounded by numerous microphones he announced, "This video clearly reveals that the testimony that had been given by the school children and Ms. Miller is accurate. This newly discovered evidence, a Digital Security Systems video recording of the hijacking of bus 51, has surfaced and it will be entered as evidence and presented to the court."

Within twenty-four hours, Mr. Bilford Lorring came to the station and watched the video, "I will be talking to the parents of Billy Culpepper and Jack Weller and let them know of the video. I'm sure the parents will drop the charges on Sarah Miller. In addition, the parents will probably withdraw the lawsuit against the County School System."

Slater was bound and determined to see that the extraordinary courage of the bus driver and heroic efforts of Dannie HD Macon were going to the press. He set a date, time, and place to have HD, Billy, Jack, Sarah, and the Big Banyan Reservation trail runners tell their story.

Once the newly surfaced video evidence clearly vindicating Sarah Miller was made public, Slater knew it would be safe for Sarah to go home. "I must admit I am sorry to see you go. You can stay and should for another week or so. You still need medical care." Slater wanted to add, "and because I want to take care of you," but he held his tongue knowing that he was more than just a little attracted to Sarah. Maybe she sensed his affections towards her and perhaps he wasn't her type. "I'm more than ready to go home Lou, but I'm grateful for all your help," Sarah said.

"Since you insist on leaving, I'll drive you home. I've taken the liberty of arranging for a nurse to stay with you, she will be with you for as long as you need her, day and night, what with the seriousness of that chest wound and well the nightmares you are having—it is good to not be alone."

****

I am not myself right now. Lou Slater's offer to relieve me of having to think more than beyond the moment was well received and I *am* grateful. Getting back to my own home will help me recover from the past weeks. I think of the children every day, and hope they are doing better than I am. I can hear Billy's voice in my sleep, and I miss him. But his little boy's voice is not the only one I hear, the mean voices are there too. But, according to Emily, the psychiatric post traumatic nurse Slater hired for me, the voices will, in time, fade away along with the nightmares and, the gunshot wound which I am beginning to think will never heal—completely.

Emily helped me cope and find ways to think my way out of the brutal hijacking I endured. With no one else to fall back on, Emily had become a great comfort to me.

Then, one day out of the blue, I got an invitation to HD's high school graduation. Due to the shooting at the school last May, the graduation was postponed until now, August. I was amazed how something like an invitation to a high school graduation lifted my spirits.

CHAPTER 37

Two months after the bus hijacking, Slater
received a call from Tommy Storm Macon,

"Officer Slater my wife and I would like you
to join us at HD's high school graduation."

"I would be honored! Tommy, I have to say
it feels good to not be forgotten by the people I
serve, thanks for the invite!"

When Slater arrived at the high school
auditorium, he found Sarah sitting next to Billy
and his parents, Jack, and his mom, all of HD's
family and friends, the trail runners, and Paul
Bowman, they all sat in a row in the auditorium,
at the end of the row was an empty chair
reserved for Slater. He went down the row and
shook hands with everyone before he sat down.

It was a typical high school graduation until
HD was called to receive his diploma. The
entire auditorium stood up and cheered and
clapped for five minutes. HD didn't just
graduate with honors and a scholarship to the
school of his choice, he was applauded as a hero
by his peers. HD was not just Billy and Jack's
hero, he was their hero too. In a way, the
applause for HD was a show of hope for all the

kids and a purging of the violence and great loss from the random shooter who killed students earlier in the year.

Up until now, Slater had never seen the graduating senior smile. He hadn't looked at HD with attention to detail. Today, however, as HD walked on stage to accept his diploma, he stood tall. A broad-shouldered youth with pitch black hair and a burnished tan against his blushing face. What touched Slater most was his quiet dignity. HD was totally unaware of how much he was appreciated. Jack and Billy waved and jumped up and down as they cheered for him. Jack whistled and cheered some more, "Over here, over here!" Jack shouted until HD saw him.

After receiving his diploma, HD waved to them all. Slater was grateful for being invited to share in this moment with HD, his friends and family.

CHAPTER 38

I decided to resume my job as a bus driver for the school system. They welcomed me back and I might add, they honored me as a local hero of sorts. Being honored and resuming my job felt good and I haven't felt good since the hijacking. However, I'm not out of the woods yet.

I'm bound and determined to overcome an all-consuming residual fear that is the aftermath of my time in the military and the nightmare in Flamingo. I decided to resume target practice twice a week at the local firing range. I'm intent on keeping my sharpshooter skills 'sharp.' As a civilian, I know that kind of thinking is questionable not to mention paranoid. While I was vigilant with the physical therapy required to regain strength and mobility, I still had difficulty holding my handgun steady.

Emily, my psych nurse, concluded her time with me. She was confident that I could function well in day-to-day activities. At first, I just wanted to be left alone and that left me wide open to moments of uncontrollable anxiety. But I've gradually learned to manage my fears—alone. My job as bus driver for the school system (that I originally considered beneath my intelligence) now, gives me great comfort. I love the children on the bus. Being around them, hearing their laughter and joy—well there are those occasions of misbehavior, but overall, I look forward to getting up in the morning. I have also become better acquainted with Lou Slater. Over the past few months, I got to know him better.

He has this ability to see through me. Despite that uncomfortable feeling, he has helped me. He recommended that I seek psychiatric help, and I did so, resentfully at first. So, now I sit amongst others with similar emotional issues in group therapy sessions. The therapist said that the sessions would help me to become comfortable around people. He was right and the sessions proved to be a big help. If anything, I realized I'm not as alone as I thought I was.

Some of the meetings were unpleasant. On occasion, people broke down and cried, others exhibited anger and frustration as their lives were rankled by trauma. One day, my therapist asked me if I had been back to Flamingo since the hijacking. His question took me aback. It was as though he asked me if I had a nightmare, stuck pins in my eyeballs, or some other macabre activity.

However, the therapist presented Flamingo in a most inviting way, "It's a quiet tranquil place, fishing boats come and go at the Flamingo Marina throughout the late fall and winter months as they are the best months to visit the Everglades National Park. It is quite popular amongst bird watchers, naturalists, fishermen and hunters. The Marina and the Flamingo ghost town campgrounds are indeed still very much part of the park," he continued "it's just that the campgrounds are deserted, maybe someday they will reopen."

"For me, it's a place with a real bad memory and, no, I have no intention of ever going back there," I was not happy with his questions, "why would you ask me that, why would you say — have I ever been back?"

"Because trauma can emotionally cripple you," the therapist answered, "if we all go through life being afraid of a place because something bad happened to us, most of us would probably never come out of our houses."

I came away from that meeting uncomfortable and edgy. I wanted to do the right thing. So, I considered a trip to Flamingo but certainly not alone. I hoped Jack or Billy would consider a day outing with me. As it turned out, Billy's parents strongly negated the idea of him going back to *that place*. His folks felt that he needed more time to get over the trauma of it all. I wondered if it was the same with Jack or HD.

Thinking about it just made me want a double shot of vodka. Then, I thought of Lou Slater. Maybe I should ask him to go with me to Flamingo, after all it was his idea for me to get professional help in the first place. I still felt awkward and nervous around him. He has such a big presence. I'm just not ready for the kind of attention Slater wanted to give me, especially since I still loved my deceased husband.

HD and his parents had invited me to dinner a few times and we took a liking to each other. I felt comfortable around them, and I felt safe. So, I decided to give Tommy and Mary Macon a call. "I was wondering if you might like to go with me, you know, like a day outing to one of the places in the glades. I understand there are picnic areas there."

"We would love to join you!"

We decided on a visit the day before Thanksgiving. Mary Dove Macon had arranged for HD to join us as he was home for the holiday. In turn, he contacted Jack's mother and asked her if Jack could join us. They also arranged for the trail runners/trackers to join us as well. Then, Mary Dove invited me to Thanksgiving dinner. She would not take no for an answer.

No matter how I rationalized and implemented anxiety-free thinking techniques, the upcoming trip to Flamingo became a constant obsession. I continued the therapy sessions in the hope that it would provide some relief even if only during the meetings. The last thing I wanted to do was start drinking every night, again.

I decided to learn more about Big Banyan Reservation's history, which also included HD's heritage. I already knew he was Native American. I reluctantly agreed to meet up with HD at the home of Denis Watergrass, the lead trail runner who rescued us last summer and whom I barely remembered. It surprised me to learn that Denis lived at the Big Banyan Reservation, a place and community that I never knew existed prior to my decision to do some research.

Denis laid out the entire history of Big Banyan Reservation, one of seven reservations in Florida and home to many Native Americans who are collectively known as the Seminole Nation and whose translation, "renegade," is a word that grouped numerous American Indian tribes into one community at the turn of the 20th century. Today, they are collectively known as the Seminole Nation.

No history book in my schools ever spoke of the Seminole Nation. The Florida State University in Tallahassee, Florida named their sports teams after the Seminoles—but I knew nothing about these Floridians.

Anyway, my decision to do a little research on the reservations proved to be a good idea. I was stunned at what I had learned. I found myself curious about my own ancestry. Aside from being a widow and childless, I was an only child. My parents died over ten years ago, so I'd have to research our family name myself.

It amazed me that the American Indian community traced their lineage back hundreds of years, in oral tradition no less. Tourists who visited the Florida reservations knew more about the Seminoles than I did, a lifelong resident of Monroe County! I began to appreciate my new friends more and I looked forward to my time with HD's family.

Maybe they have planned a cook-out, a Seminole Indian dance performance or perhaps they plan a tour of their museum. A day on a river that spanned much of my home state, through miles of river grass was the last thing I imagined.

A week before the big event I received a visitor. One evening while reading one of several of my self-help books, there was a firm knock on the door.

"I need a break anyway," I said to myself as I got up to answer the door. "Hold on I'm coming, no need to knock the door down."

I flipped the outdoor light on and opened the door. Slater, bigger than life as usual, stood outside my door. "I never realized how tall you are Lou, till just now," I said, a smile spread across my face, "what's that you have there?"

With all his macho, cool presence, Slater stood at the door with a vulnerable look upon his face. Peeking out of the crook of his arm was a puppy. "Not that it matters what breed this little fella is," Slater said with a bit of a stammer, "the object of my visit is to bring you a special someone that I think would be a good addition to your life."

"For me?" I say surprised, "what am I supposed to do with a puppy?"

"Love it, you never know what a little tender loving pup will do for you."

Without asking, Slater entered my house and handed me the little pup. I juggled the wiggly puppy in my arms. It licked my face incessantly. Slater went out to his car and returned with a dog crate, a bag of puppy food and puppy toys. He set the crate up in the kitchen. "When they're little, like this, it's good to keep them in an area where the floors are bare," Slater advised, "you can put a puppy gate up at the doorway there," he said as he pointed to the kitchen doorway, "that will keep him confined until he's old enough not to chew up your house."

Slater went to the kitchen and set up the puppy crate. He set a litter tray in the back of the crate along with some newspapers, then he scattered a few puppy toys in the crate for the pup to chew on. After a few moments, Slater looked at me and smiled, "Now you're all set. Just feed him once in the morning and once at night, make sure he has plenty of water and take him out for walks several times a day."

I was too astonished to respond and looked back and forth from Slater to the puppy whose adoring eyes and little puppy kisses had already stolen my heart, "Thank you, Slater, I don't know what to say."

"He'll be a fine friend," Slater nodded, "take him down to the dog park a few blocks from here," Slater suggested, "that's where I take my dog."

"You have a dog?

"Uh, well as a matter of fact I do have a dog, the pup's mother. This pup's the last of the litter. Maybe we'll see each other at the dog park someday," Slater said as he handed me a sheet of paper. "Here's some info on the pup. Just so you know he's an English bulldog. Here's the phone number of the Vet whose giving him puppy shots. You'll have to take him to the Vet for the rest of his shots."

We looked back and forth at each other and the pup. There was an awkward silence between us. Then I said, "Thank you, Lou, for thinking of me, I really appreciate your thoughtfulness." I smiled, "I'm sure we'll see each other at the dog park."

When Slater left the house, I noticed there was a bit of a bounce to his step. I felt that maybe he thought I was holding out, that maybe I would come around. He cared for me more than I imagined and yes, giving me the pup was a stroke of genius when it came to winning my heart.

I looked down at my newfound friend, "Now what am I supposed to do with the likes of you, little fella, gotta give you a name, hmm, how 'bout I call you— Little Lou, after that man who's driving away in his truck."

CHAPTER 39

The following week, I decided to bring the pup to work. I put his crate behind the driver's seat and as each child boarded the bus in the morning, a look of delight spread across their faces as they greeted Lil Lou. When the kids got off the bus in the afternoon, they'd all take a second to say goodbye to the pup. Before long, anxiety attacks that had plagued me since the hijacking begin to subside, thanks to the therapy sessions, my new friends, Lou Slater, and Lil Lou.

I debated as to whether I should bring the pup to the reservation with me the Wednesday before Thanksgiving. I hated leaving him in his crate, but I knew if I left him to roam the house for any length of time that I'd return to a shredded home! So, I decided to leave him with Slater.

I packed up all his gear, drove out to Slater's house and set Lil' Lou's crate down at Slater's front door. I knew he'd take good care of the pup. I left a note letting Slater know that I'd be back for the pup the next day. I patted Lil Lou's head, "When I get back, I'll take you for a nice long walk, I promise." My pup looked up at me expectantly.

On the day of the everglades outing, I picked up the Chief of Police, Paul Bowman. After a few pleasant words of greeting, I drove to Big Banyan Reservation to meet up with several soon to be new friends. I pulled into a gravel parking lot adjacent to the Calusa Boat Landing. I had no idea what was in store for me, and I was surprised that I wasn't wringing my hands with anxiety, which usually occurred when I didn't know what was going to happen.

I recognized Jack and HD among the few men who stood around the Landing. However, I didn't recognize anyone else and assumed they were HD's friends. HD turned and smiled at me; I walked toward him with open arms and hugged the young college freshman.

"College suits you HD," I said, "look at you, quite the young man." I reached up and touched his cheek, "Hurricane Dove," I whispered, such that only HD can hear me. He looked down at me, a sadness in his eyes.

***

HD had a flashback of memory, he recalled—
the first time Sarah called him by his native
name. She was propped against a gumbo limbo
tree, bleeding from a gunshot wound and in and
out of consciousness, struggling to breathe and
in pain. HD quickly smiled and said, "Billy
can't make it; he and his parents are out of town
for the holiday. Let me introduce you to some
people whom you may remember from my
graduation."

HD turned and motioned for the men to
approach them, "Sarah this is Denis Watergrass,
Mark Morris, and Sheriff Bowman's sons, Joel
and Chris Bowman. These guys tracked us all
the way to the deserted Flamingo campsite.
They ran the old trails south from Big Banyan
Reservation and over the Wilderness Waterway
where they picked up our trail at Bear Lake.
They found us at the old Flamingo campsite and
accompanied us from the campsite to the
Marina. You may not remember them, you
know, you were in bad shape."

***

HD continued to tell me how they jimmied the lock of the Marina store and hid there during the gun fight across the street at the Visitor's Center. He told me how desperate they were to get medical treatment for me and how all of them, except Billy, went for help.

"He wouldn't leave your side and right before we left you and Billy, he was sitting on the floor against the back wall his arms around you, your head cradled in his lap."

As HD spoke, I began to remember snippets of activity that occurred that time in the Marina. HD continued, "You saved Billy's life that night, and mortally wounded one of the bank robbers who kidnapped the bus."

"No need to remind me of that recurring nightmare."

As HD continued to talk, a tightness in my gut rose at the memory of those hours in the Marina, "You saved us, HD, if it hadn't been for you," I said, "we would've all died at the hands of those men."

"Not so," HD insisted, "we all helped each other through that ordeal, that was the miracle of it all, I could not have done it alone. When

Billy collapsed in fear and exhaustion, it was Jack who carried him—for miles, in the pitch black of that second night, as we walked Flamingo Road, it was Jack who suspected the truck driver as one of the gunmen at the Visitor Center. I was sure he was a night-fishermen, why else would he have appeared out of nowhere. But Jack guessed right, God knows where that man would have taken us. As it turned out, the truck driver was one of the guys who hijacked us. We pulled him from the burning truck, carried him until the helicopter showed up that rushed him to the hospital. I hear he died anyway. Word is he died on a bus, somewhere near the Keys. Imagine the irony of that, he died on a bus! We made it through that terror helping each other and you were there for Billy so many times. We all helped each other through those two terrifying nights in the glades."

No one said anything for a moment, then Denis coughed and said, "Listen, time to board the airboat, we have some wonderful things we want to show you, Sarah."

"What a contraption! Has anyone ever fallen off this boat?" I gasped as I had never seen an airboat before today. Wide open sides padded long seats and what looked like a huge fan was attached to what I learned was an airboat. "Let me introduce to you my boat, Nellie," Denis said, "this here is what I call the Trail Runner, it's an 18x18 diamondback airboat, with a 496 CID engine, with 425 HP, a belt drive of CH3.3:1 and the prop is a 4-blade carbon fiber wide stainless-steel powder coated rig. A quarter inch polymer shield is screwed on side by side for a rear operator—and" Denis smiled from ear to ear, "that would be me! And these gauges on the center instrument panel are made of carbon fiber. In addition, we have two 4-man passenger seats which means there is room for all of us."

Denis took his place in the operator's seat at the rear and turned the key. The boat revved up and was ready to go. Jack was the first to jump aboard, Joel and Chris helped me aboard, followed by HD. Mark, Chris, and Joel took their places in the second row of seats.

"Buckle up Jack," I said, a little fear in my voice tone. Denis backed the airboat away from the landing and turned it around. He accelerated just enough to smoothly glide through the waterway that had a thick dense canopy of mangroves on either side of the sliver of water. It was shady as we passed through the tangled jungle, but it wasn't long before the mangroves grew sparse. Soon the airboat approached a wide-open space, and the mangroves were behind us. Ahead was a breathtaking expanse of bright blue sky. Denis accelerated again and the air boat picked up speed. The waterway was filled with one of the oldest plants in the world, a tall sawgrass, a hardy species of sedge with long green folds, that were outlined with fine razor-sharp saw teeth. The sawgrass stretched as far as the eye could see.

HD pointed westward, "The everglades are often referred to as a river of grass. Over there are numerous small islands. I know people who live there. Their families go back more years and generations than has ever been recorded. To the east, are the mangroves just like the ones back at the landing. Between those mangroves and this waterway is the hammock. The very one that we walked through by way of the center trail which is cut right down the middle of the hammock. That trail, Ms. Sarah, led us directly to the Flamingo campgrounds on the shores of Florida Bay. You may recall the feral hog and," HD paused for a second, "the green anaconda—it was half in and half out of the trail."

"No, I don't remember that at all," I said.

***

HD reflected on the gruesome sight of the feral hog being squeezed to death by a huge green anaconda. The snake's mouth was full of sharp inward slanted teeth. It had a death bite on the hogs' neck and its predatory beady eyes followed us as we walked past. "No, I'm not going to tell her that, I still have nightmares of that huge snake glaring at me from the foot of my bed. No, I'm not going to tell her about that," HD muttered to himself.

"I heard that," Sarah said, her voice tone full of factual interest "was it a big snake?"

"Well yes, the green anaconda is not from around here, it was released in the Everglades by people who let their 'pets' loose after they got bored with them or when the snake got too big for its owner's city environment. Now we have the anaconda and another predatory snake, the Burmese python swimming all over the glades. They compete with the alligators and crocodiles for prey. The two species of snake are so powerful that the crocs and gators have been known to fall victim to them. We have had hunters come back from the glades with reports of a huge anaconda or python wrapped around a gator in a death grip," HD said.

A few feet from the air boat, a flock of little blue herons flew out of the saw grass and away from the air boat as it passed by. Sarah was surprised at their sudden appearance and smiled to see such a sight. Denis slowed the air boat as they came to a crossroads in the wide channel of water.

He turned the boat west away from the hammock and then went south again to another narrower way. Here, the water was deeper and clearer, the edges of the narrow water way were dense with hyacinths and other colorful water weeds. Live oaks lined the river's edge, and a diversity of fern trimmed the trunks of the banyan trees, Florida boxwoods, and red-brown gumbo limbo trees.

***

I had a flash of memory. I remember leaning against the trunk of one of those large trees. HD had hovered over me. He'd made a paste from some leaves and applied it around the gunshot wound. "I'm not gonna cry," I whispered to myself, as the air boat cruised smoothly through the river. There's was no mistaking the gumbo-limbo tree. It stood amongst other trees I'd never seen before today. HD pointed out the ilex, eugenias and poisonwood trees. "Some of these trees are not originally indigenous to the Everglades," HD explained, "the seeds were carried over from Caribbean islands and across the ocean by way of hurricanes.

HD pointed upwards to the higher branches of the trees; there in great abundance, pastel yellow and white orchids hung in what appeared to be suspended animation among the treetops. "I didn't know that orchids grow like that," I said amazed at the sight.

As Denis commandeered the air boat further south towards the beaches of Florida Bay and the ghost town of Flamingo campgrounds, the great royal palms appeared in magnificent clusters along the southernmost part of the hammock, as did the stands of silver palms and finally, the coconut palms came into view, the closer we came to the Bay.

The landscape was gradually changing. Some of the cypress trees, that flourished in the northern fresh waters of the Everglades grew to 120 feet tall and gradually gave way to the cypress with gnarly root-like extensions called cypress knees, that grew clear down to the saltwater of Florida Bay. "Many places in Florida are named after these cypress trees," HD explained, "they're everywhere here in the glades."

To the east of the waterway, I noticed something rustling around in the dry grasses of the hammock, "What's going on out there?"

Mark, Joel, and Chris, who were sitting behind me, laughed and hooted, "It's a great place for hunting," Mark said, "The game is plentiful out here, it's enough to feed the entire population of Florida. So few people know about this place. You could say the glades are a hunting ground less traveled."

HD looked out over the hammock towards the movement in the high grasses, "I'd say it's a rafter of turkeys, some would say a flock," as he points to the treetops, "Look up in the tops of the cypress, sometimes you can see where they roost."

That day I learned that Mark was an expert tracker and hunter. "There's also deer, wildcats and panthers out here," he said, "we don't hunt the panthers though. They're an endangered species, but the deer are in abundance. We have black bear out here too, but we hunt the wild hogs and compete with the anacondas and panthers for them. Mustn't forget the birds, especially the wild duck. Welcome to our world Miss Sarah."

"Indeed! There are lots of birds here! I'm amazed by it all," I said overwhelmed. For the remainder of our trip to Flamingo, I marveled at the huge community of birds; bald eagles soared high above the trees, flocks of grackles swarmed and flew everywhere. Further south, osprey soared above, their wings buoyed by the winds ever present in the glades. Joel chimed in, "Once we get close to the Bay, you will see the frigate birds, also known as Man O' War birds, big ocean birds, and they are in near constant flight, ever present throughout the tropic seas."

"Their wingspan stretches 7 ½ ft, the largest in proportion to the body of any 3-4 lb. bird," Chris said, who up until now had been silent, "and," he continued, "the sighting of the frigates is how we know we are getting close to the Florida Bay."

***

The men in the back seat of the air boat looked at each other in a somber, knowing way. They wondered how Sarah would respond to a visit to a place that could only be described as her nightmare in hell. "Think she'll remember being laid out on the concrete picnic table?" Mark whispered, "of course, she was in and out of consciousness, so she may not remember the time at the campgrounds."

"I don't know. I'm not sure I'd forget being carried the extra six miles to the Marina in the pitch black of night," Joel said, "I wonder how she will react to the next few hours of the trip."

"Well, we'll just have to wait and see," Chris said under his breath.

Meanwhile, Sarah was caught up in the flurry of thousands of sandpipers and ducks that passed by overhead. Each species flew within its' own flock formation. Minutes before Denis docked the airboat at the campgrounds, white pelicans whose magnificent wingspan measured nearly ten feet from wing tip to wing tip, soared silently over the crashing waves of the Florida Bay. The trail runners were relieved to see that Sarah appeared smitten by the beauty of their glades.

Denis brought the air boat into the landing's shallow waters and secured the ropes on a docking post. From the landing it was a short walk to Flamingo's deserted campgrounds. The aroma of grilled hamburgers, and sausages filled the air. Tommy Storm Macon and his wife Mary Dove, along with Police Chief Bowman, surprised everyone with a cookout near the very place the trail runners found HD, Sarah, Billy, and Jack, on that harrowing night back in June.

There were several coolers of iced sodas and beers on one of the picnic tables. Everyone made a bee line to the coolers, and someone turned on a boom box. Within minutes laughter and music echoed through the empty ruined campgrounds.

CHAPTER 40

I helped Mary set the food out on the table. I totally enjoyed the cookout. I was oblivious to any bad memories my newfound friends thought I might experience. In fact, I felt happy. I hadn't felt this happy since before my husband died. I was grateful to be amongst HD's friends and family. As the day wore on, strong winds kicked up over Florida Bay that heralded the late afternoon tides. I said to Mary, "It's a beautiful sight out there, let's check out some shells."

"No, you go ahead, I want to finish putting things away."

I walked down to the shoreline and picked up a conch shell. Its interior was a beautiful pink and just as I was about to put it to my ear to listen to roaring waves echo through the inner shell chamber, HD came up behind me. "I don't think that's a good idea Miss Sarah, there just might be a crab living in the shell. Not that it would come out and bite you or anything, well maybe, but you should know that the conch shells have living things in them."

"Oh, thanks for letting me know, stupid me," I laughed, "should have known about the crab in the shell! Okay then, good to know that."

"Yo! HD you comin' with us or not?" Denis hollered, "times a wastin' and we have turkeys to hunt for dinner tomorrow."

"I'm coming too!"

"I'll see you tomorrow, Miss Sarah. Mom and Dad will take you home." HD said as he and Jack quickly boarded as Denis revved up the airboat.

I watched after Jack, HD, and his friends as the airboat motored out of sight.

"Let's get going Sarah," Tommy said, "I want to stop at the Marina on our way out. The fishing boats will be docking very soon, I want to get there before the best of their haul is sold."

We drove a few miles to Flamingo Visitor Center and Marina. I felt carefree and relaxed, still in the glow of the great day outing. When we arrived at the Marina, there were cars parked out front. Men were unloading coolers filled with their catch of the day. Fishing boats lined the docked at the pier. People milled around as the fishermen lay out a variety of fish on tables filled with crushed ice.

"Let's go get some fish," Tommie said, "before it's all bought up."

"I've never seen such an array of fresh fish, is that a sea bass?"

"Good guess! A good five pounder too, grab some paper towels over there" Mary said, "and get your fish before someone else grabs it!"

I picked up a lively wriggling fish in the paper towels, but it slipped out and I had to grab it in my bare hands before it flipped back into the water. I gave the fish to a man who filleted it, wrapped it in butchers' paper and handed it back to me. I looked at Mary and said, "Can you hold my fish for me, I've gotta' wash my hands, I'll be right back."

I was so not used to holding a live fish in my bare hands and was relieved there was a place where I could wash my hands. I went inside the Marina store and walked towards the back of the store where the restrooms were located. The bait and tackle store smelled of dry old wood, the floorboards creaked beneath me as I made my way to the back of the Marina. When I finished washing my hands, my forehead was beaded with sweat, my hands trembled, my heart pounded in my chest and my stomach tightened. I had suddenly realized the shop was familiar to me. The smell of the place set off an anxiety attack. I slowly opened the restroom door and looked past the shelves of merchandise.

Straight across the back wall of the Marina was a room with OFFICE written above the door frame. To the right of the office was a window that looked out at the faded, mildewed Visitor Center. Right there, under the window, yes, I remembered sitting there telling Billy to go hide under the desk in the office. There were no boxes by the window today. The night I sat against it there were boxes I had hidden behind and rested a rifle on. Then, I shot a man. I saved Billy's life that night.

A calm came over me. I felt as though my husband stood next to me. Of course, he wasn't here. He'd been dead some time now, a casualty of the Afghan war. But the calm I felt was the same kind of calm I always felt when he was with me. I looked down at that spot where I sat against the wall. Yes, I did the right thing. Just as I'd done the right thing a few years back in Afghanistan, where I'd sit atop the hummers and trucks in convoy ready to take out the enemy. The anxiety began to subside, I took a deep breath, "I'm okay."

I left the Marina store and caught up with Mary and Tommy. "Let's go. You brought me here on purpose, didn't you?" Mary and Tommy nodded yes. They looked at me, a knowing look in their eyes. "I reckon there's a good chance I can get past that nightmare." I gave them each a hug, "I'm glad you brought me here, thanks."

"It was a gamble," Tommy said, his face a mix of compassion and worry, "but we thought it would help you put the whole mess behind you."

"Tommie lets go home," Mary said as she nodded to me, "and cook up some fish."

"Yea, Tommie," I said, "let's do."

"It was HD's idea to bring you here," Mary said, "he didn't think it was right for you to go the rest of your life hating a place like the Everglades, he didn't want you to go through the rest of your life—hating his backyard.

"Yea," I said, "I recall him saying that to me once—that the glades were his backyard. He said that just before we all took off through the glades to Flamingo. He knew we were all scared to death, and he said that to give us some comfort."

When I got home that night, Lil Lou was excited to see me, and I was glad to be home. I felt tired and wonderful at the same time; the fish was delicious not like the three-day old fish sold at the grocery store. For the first time in a long time, I went to bed that night without a 'sleep aide.'

The holiday season turned out to be the best I'd had in a long time. I felt like an adopted member of HD's family, and I was sure Jack, and his mother felt that way too. When the semester was out for the year, HD spent a lot of time with Jack, who now referred to HD as 'bro.'

CHAPTER 41

It's been ten months since the bus was hijacked.
I'm feeling good these days. When I get up in
the morning, I'm quick to shower and dress for
the day. Without a second thought, I always
strap on my holster and handgun, it's against the
rules to carry a gun on the school bus but it's
under my baggy shirt and so long as I have a
license to carry, I'm never going to be without
it. I feel safer armed. The next time someone
knocks on my bus door and points a gun at me, I
will shoot first and ask questions later. Maybe
not, maybe I need more therapy. I know that
even though he is away at college, HD still
wears his hunting knife strapped to his leg,
under his jeans.

With the help of the trail runners who are
now Jack's hunting mentors, the young teen was
out most weekends with one or more of them
and had mastered the bow and arrow. I've been
told some animals can only be hunted with a
bow and arrow in the glades. Jack also owns a
brand-new hunting rifle and bowie knife like
HD's. I'm told Jack can hit a target bull's eye
from fifty feet with that bowie knife.

My bulldog, Lil Lou, is almost full grown now, my constant companion and best buddy. Today, I was cutting back overgrown branches of azaleas that profusely bloom this time of year, (in fact everything around Florida City was in full bloom, as spring comes early here), when a vehicle pulled up to the house. I figured it was the mailman but instead of moving down the road to the next house I heard a car door slam shut. I wondered if the postman had a delivery for me. I don't recall ordering anything.

I heard my front gate open, and I turned around. Nope, no postman, rather it was Lou Slater and a beautiful female bulldog in a pink harness and leash walked beside him. "Thought I'd drop by," Lou said, "and see how you and the pup are doing."

"Well, hey, what a delightful surprise and who is this little gal?"

"This here happens to be your dog's mother."

"As you can see, Lil Lou is doing quite well.

"Lil Lou, huh," Slater laughed, "I'll take that as a compliment!"

"In answer to your question, things are going well. I got my job back, driving the bus for school. Lil Lou comes to work with me, in fact, he is the high school, junior high and elementary school mascot. He's quite popular with the kids."

"I see," Slater said with a smile and a nod, "what do you hear from HD, Jack and Billy?"

"HD is doing very well. He's in his second semester in college. Jack and his mother have been practically adopted by HD's family, and from what I hear from the elementary school, Billy's family moved south towards Miami. He attends Logan School for the Gifted, and I hear he's doing quite well."

Slater and I talked for a while. I finally got up the nerve to invite Slater to dinner. Slater was quick to accept the invitation. The next thing I know is we were seeing each other regularly to walk the dogs and spend time doing other things good friends do.

I never thought I'd fall in love again but here I was falling in love, and it was okay. I don't feel guilty about it. I'm sure my late husband would approve of Slater.

One evening Billy Culpepper (now 9 years old), was featured on the local evening news.

He'd won a ribbon for catching a large barracuda at the local Miami Dade Junior Fishing tournament. An interviewing reporter asked Billy, "Is this your most exciting catch?"

"This is a big fish," Billy said, quick to respond, "and to look at it you can see it's a monster what with all those teeth. But it's not the only monster fish I've ever caught. The first monster fish I ever caught was a peacock bass, the ugliest fish I ever saw, a real monster fish if you ask me…"

The reporter gently tried to take back the microphone while Billy exclaimed over the monster fish that he caught in the glades at Bear Lake last summer.

I could still hear Billy talking about the monster fish in the background as the news reporter attempted to sign off.

Cast of Characters.

Dannie Hurricane Dove Macon aka HD-
18-year-old senior at Florida City High
School, Native American, member of the
Seminole Nation, on Bus 51 the day it was
hijacked.

Jack Weller- 13-year-old seventh grader, on
Bus 51 the day it was hijacked.

Billy Culpepper- 8-year-old second grader,
on Bus 51 the day it was hijacked.

Sarah Miller-Veteran, Former US Army
Sergeant, served in Afghanistan, convoy driver,
gunner, wounded warrior, widow, and bus
driver of Bus 51 the day it was hijacked.

Kyle Moleto
Ben Sykes
Eddie Ringold
Three recent college graduates, aka thieves,
murderers, kidnapers, bank robbers and
hijackers of Bus 51

Tommie Storm Macon
Mary Dove Macon
Native American, parents of HD

Deputy Chuck Hillert- Monroe County Deputy
Deputy Rudy Pepper- Monroe County Deputy
Deputy Jimmy Danner- Monroe County

Lou Slater- Chief Deputy Monroe County

Sheriff John Hampstead- Monroe County Sheriff

Detective Morris- Detective with Dade County Police

Paul Bowman- Police Chief, Big Banyan Reservation

George Russell- FBI Agent in charge of bank robbery investigation

Ronnie Tigertail- HD's second cousin

Jamey Johns- Member of Big Banyan Tribal Council in charge of Emergency Management

Paul Myers- In charge of 1 of 3 broadcasting stations at Big Banyan Reservation.

Denis Watergrass
Mark Morris
Joel and Chris Bowman
Known as the Trail Runners, expert game hunters and trackers of the Florida Everglades, tracked Sarah, HD, Jack, and Billy from Bear Lake to Flamingo ghost town campgrounds.

Ms. Milli Weller- single parent and mother to Jack Weller

William & Ellie Culpepper- Parents of Billy Culpepper

Bob Darnell- tournament fisherman

Bob Brotelle- Employee at Tamiami Gas and Shop, witness to jeep and bus along Route 41.

Doctor Matt Fry- Monroe County Coroner

Mary Louise Pettigrew- Manager at Monroe County Digital Security Systems

Attorney Bilford Lorring- Attorney hired by Jack Weller's and Billy Culpepper's parents to prosecute Sarah Miller for child endangerment, violation of County school bus regulations.

Peggy Sue Sykes- Ben Sykes sister, who hid the bus video of the hijacking.